Breakfast with Paul

two novellas, two survivors

Breakfast with Paul © 2023 Bernard Marin

All Rights Reserved. No part of this book may be reproduced in any form or by any electronic or mechanical means including information storage and retrieval systems, without permission in writing from the author. The only exception is by a reviewer, who may quote short excerpts in a review.

This book is a work of fiction and creative non-fiction. Names, characters, places, and incidents are either products of the author's imagination or are used fictitiously. Any resemblance to actual persons, living or dead, events, or locales is entirely coincidental.

Printed in Australia
Cover and internal design by Shawline Publishing Group Pty Ltd

First printing: September 2023

Shawline Publishing Group Pty Ltd
www.shawlinepublishing.com.au

Paperback ISBN 978-1-9228-5032-4
eBook ISBN 978-1-9228-5037-9

Distributed by Shawline Distribution and Lightning Source Global

 A catalogue record for this work is available from the National Library of Australia

More great Shawline titles can be found by scanning the QR code below.
New titles also available through Books@Home Pty Ltd.
Subscribe today at www.booksathome.com.au or scan the QR code below.

Breakfast with Paul

two novellas, two survivors

Bernard Marin

Also by Bernard Marin:

My Father, my Father

Good as Gold

Stories of Profit and Loss

Stories of Remembering and Forgetting

Letter to my Father

People Who Have Changed the World: Imagined Interviews

We Had a Dream: Stories from the Civil Rights Movement

These titles can be found at bernardmarin.com.au

Contents

Breakfast with Paul: We Beg to Differ.. 1
1 Maralinga 5
2 Nazi Collaborators 20
3 Reaganomics 29
4 IBM and the Holocaust 38
5 The House Un-American Activities Committee 53
6 The Julius Rosenwald Schools 66
7 Hitler's Judiciary 78
8 The Mitford Sisters 89
9 The Letter 99

Surviving: My Story 105
Author's Note 107

About the Author 169

Acknowledgments

I was privileged to have the assistance of many people while writing this story. I am grateful for the help of Nan McNab. Her extensive work in editing these stories has been instrumental in making them infinitely better. I have greatly benefited from her insights, guidance and assistance. I owe her a huge debt of gratitude for her incredibly generous support. I am truly grateful to her. She gave willingly of her time and has been remarkably patient with me. Nothing was too difficult, and she was a pleasure to work with.

My heartfelt thanks to Bob Sessions for his support and guidance. His astute and constructive comments have been most valuable. He has been a source of great insight and I owe him a huge debt of gratitude for his invaluable assistance. He gave willingly of his time and I have benefited from his understanding, acumen and direction.

I have also benefited from the endless hours of typing and retyping by Noni Carr-Howard.

Finally, many friends have been there for me along this journey. They are too numerous to name—you know who you are. Thank you for your support and encouragement. And last but not least, thank you to my family for your enthusiastic support and for helping me keep everything in perspective.

Breakfast with Paul

We Beg to Differ

Dedication

For my wife, Wendy; daughters, Amy and Rachel;
daughter-in-law, Deb, and son-in-law, Joel;
and grandchildren, Goldie, Ziggy and Millie

*In memory of those who were lost
and those who survived the Holocaust*

1
Maralinga

'How are you?' Paul said as the waiter brought his breakfast. 'Excuse my ordering – I'm starving.' We were at Darling Street Café, our regular place for breakfast on Saturday mornings.

Paul and I were close friends. In our youth we had been inseparable. He was the brother I never had, and perhaps I filled a similar role for him. We'd met at University High School and from that time on we shared secrets and confidences about everything, except his childhood in Warsaw prior to and during the war. He refused to talk about that.

Now, as retired surgeons in our eighties, we had been meeting at the same café for breakfast each Saturday for as long as I could remember. We talked about almost everything from the state of the economy and movies, to overseas travel. And today nothing had changed.

Paul was a good deal taller than me, with broad shoulders, and in contrast to my regular, rounded features, his face seemed to have been cut from stone. Cheekbones, nose, jaw and chin were made of hard, jutting lines, and his mouth was wide and thin-lipped. His eyes were dark and deep set, and his iron-grey hair was long, thick and wavy, whereas mine was straight and a pale grey. The hair on the back of his long hands was still dark, as were his lashes and brows. I had a half inch scar on my right cheek, a souvenir of a university hockey game, but despite all Paul had gone through, he carried no visible scars.

'Well, I'm pissed off,' I said, sitting down opposite him.

'I can see that; your colour's up. What's going on?'

'Menzies has a lot to answer for!'

'Uh oh, what's set you off this time?' Paul asked.

'It was a Paul Kelly's song actually, about Maralinga…'

'And?'

'It reminded me of everything that happened and it started to play on my mind.'

'So, you googled it,' Paul said. 'Of course, you did. I know you too well.'

'And so I googled it. Our memories are not carved in stone; they often play tricks on us. Sometimes we forget, other times we distort reality.'

'Too true,' Paul said in a thin, dry voice.

I caught the waiter's eye and ordered my usual.

'Even so, the story of Maralinga is impossible to forget,' I said.

'Why do you say that? What did you discover?' Paul leaned back in his chair, his tall, thin frame only slightly stooped. He was humouring me.

'Menzies never should have allowed it.'

'What?' He quirked an eyebrow, his dark eyes twinkling.

'The British government testing nuclear weapons here,' I said. 'Maralinga and Emu Field in South Australia, the Monte Bello Islands off the West Australian coast… what was he thinking?'

Paul shrugged.

'The British carried out atomic tests in 1952 and 1956 at the Monte Bello Islands, and in 1953 at Emu Field north of Maralinga. It's only about 500 kilometres north of Adelaide.' I hesitated for a moment to recall the details of what I'd read.

'There were twelve major tests: three at Monte Bello, two at Emu Field and seven at Maralinga, and hundreds of minor trials that spread plutonium over a large area. By the time the tests concluded in 1963, radioactive and toxic elements had destroyed much of the land of the Anangu and Pitjantjatjara people.'

Paul pushed back his chair a little and said, 'But surely Menzies was acting in the interests of our national security?'

'More likely he was keen to show allegiance to the mother country.'

Paul shook his head. 'Don't be so cynical. Churchill wanted the UK to develop their own nuclear weapons because he thought they would be seen as a second-class nation if they had to rely on the United States for nuclear weapons. What's wrong with that?'

'That may be so, but Menzies was an arch conservative, a monarchist, and was only too happy to assist the motherland.'

Paul tucked into his breakfast, apparently indifferent to what I was saying.

'As far back as September 1950, in a phone call with Clement Attlee, Menzies agreed to nuclear testing without even referring the issue to cabinet. Then, after the UK discovered the conditions at Monte Bello and Emu Field were too remote to be workable, the Australian government granted them a huge chunk of South Australia to create an atomic weapons test site.'

'Don't forget the US had dropped the bomb on Hiroshima by then and allowing the British to test their weapons on our soil guaranteed us British protection, and probably US protection as well,' Paul said, his voice rising. He turned towards the waiter to catch his eye before continuing. 'Also, Australia did not have nuclear energy and we were looking for ways to power Australia.'

'Did you know that Menzies offered the British more land

than they requested?' I said.

'How was Menzies to know what would happen? Maralinga was remote and sparsely populated, so what did it matter if he offered a little more or less?'

I could see Paul was becoming irritated.

'The fact is, Menzies displayed a reckless disregard for the risks associated with large quantities of radioactive material being dispersed across the country without adequate safeguards.' Why could Paul not see that Menzies had been derelict in his duties as our prime minister?

'Why are you so critical of Menzies?' he said flatly. 'He achieved lots of good things.'

I burst out laughing. 'Nonsense! All he did was kick the communist can for as much as it was worth.'

Paul frowned. 'What do you mean?'

'Menzies was helped by good economic times. And, I might add, he benefited from the Labor Party's remarkable talent for shooting itself in the foot, especially where the DLP was concerned. Not to mention Arthur Calwell, who was an ineffectual leader – dour, dull and unelectable.' The waiter brought my coffee and I took a large sip.

Paul sighed. 'Irrespective of what you say, the fact is that under Menzies, Australia was safe, secure and prosperous.' He pulled at the collar of his shirt, and I could see the muscles in his neck tighten.

'Paul, not only did he give no thought to the potential consequences of allowing the British to test nuclear weapons on Australian soil, but he also committed Australian combat troops to fight in Vietnam when he didn't have to.'

'Have you forgotten the domino theory?' Paul said, his voice rising.

'What's to forget? It was a theory.' The waiter brought my

bagel and I took a bite, chewed, then continued. 'The US refused to allow the British to use their testing sites.'

'Yes, and for good reason!' Paul's face was flushed. 'Several British scientists had been double agents working for the Soviet Union. In 1950, Klaus Fuchs worked on the Manhattan Project, which created the first atomic bomb, and passed on secrets that helped the Soviets detonate an atom bomb years ahead of CIA projections; he confessed to being a spy!'

'That may well be, but it doesn't justify poisoning our land.'

There was a lengthy silence and I wondered if I should change the subject, but I pressed on.

'In April 1965, Menzies got up in parliament and said Australia had been asked by the South Vietnamese to send combat troops to fight in the Vietnam War. Wouldn't you think that he would have learnt from the Maralinga experience?'

'What on earth do you mean? What connection is there between Maralinga and the Vietnam War?!' Paul thumped a fist into his palm, as he often did when he was angry. 'So, what's wrong with what he said?'

'Only that it's not true!'

'Drivel!'

'There's still debate over whether Menzies really had a request from the South Vietnamese. They have always claimed that American aid was sufficient, and they didn't need any more outside help.'

Paul remained silent.

'Many people say there was no request and Menzies committed Australian combat troops purely to ingratiate himself with the US, just as he had ingratiated himself with Britain by allowing it to conduct nuclear tests on Australian soil.'

'They were our allies!' Paul rolled his eyes as if he were dealing with a simpleton.

'But all the assumptions underpinning our involvement in the Vietnam War turned out to be false. The North Vietnamese were not puppets of the Chinese, and the so-called domino theory that claimed once South Vietnam went communist, so would Thailand, Malaysia, Singapore and Indonesia, was just that, a theory. It never happened. And the massive fire power unleashed by the US on the North Vietnamese failed miserably.' I stopped for a moment to sip my water and clear my throat. 'Did you know the Vietnam War cost Australia more than five hundred lives, including about two hundred conscripts, and more than two thousand of our troops were wounded. Thousands of ex-servicemen were traumatised by the conflict, and many took their own lives. Others became seriously ill, probably due to the toxic chemicals dumped on Vietnam by the Americans.'

Paul looked uneasy, and I didn't want to upset him any more than he already was, so I said, 'I know we're strayed from what we were talking about. But the decision to allow nuclear tests on Australian soil and the decision to send combat troops to Vietnam were both the work of Menzies. He poisoned our country and our countrymen with radioactive fallout, and sent hundreds of young Australians to their deaths in a conflict we need not have joined.'

'For God's sake, the British cleaned up the sites,' said Paul, his tone one of weary patience.

'Their efforts made the contamination problems worse,' I retorted. 'The Australian government also attempted to clean up the sites in 1967, 2000 and 2009, but it left behind plutonium and other radioactive contamination.'

'What about the royal commission?'

'Sure. In 1984 there was a royal commission into the British nuclear tests, and they found that radiological hazards still remained at Maralinga.'

'Wasn't there a pretty pricey rehabilitation program?'

I shrugged. 'From memory around $100 million Australian, but what price can you put on a people's homeland?' I stared at him, but he didn't respond. 'The royal commission also found that attempts to ensure the safety of the Maralinga Tjarutja people were incompetent. The boundaries of the test fields were badly patrolled, and the British were dismissive of the safety of the Indigenous people because they regarded them as a dying race who shouldn't be allowed to influence the defence of Western civilisation.'

My sarcasm seemed lost on Paul.

'What a shockingly racist attitude. As Jews, we especially should sympathise with our Indigenous people!'

'What do you mean?'

'Our experience as Jews is, in many ways, similar to that of our Indigenous people.'

Paul gave me a quizzical look.

'The Nazis stole land from us, White Australia stole land from our Indigenous people; we, like our Indigenous people, were subjected to genocide and, like our Indigenous people, know what it is to be made victims.'

Paul gave me an uncertain look and said, 'Of course people should be judged for what they are, not for the colour of their skin or the group to which they belong. That goes without saying.'

'Thank you,' I said to the waiter as he put another coffee down for each of us. 'Did you know that the Maralinga Tjarutja people were picked up in trucks and forcibly removed from their traditional lands in the lead-up to the tests?' I hesitated a moment and swallowed some hot coffee. 'Their relocation destroyed their traditional lifestyle and culture, and because of their strong attachment to the land, this event is now embedded in their memory.'

Paul shook his head in disbelief.

'About 1200 Indigenous people were exposed to radiation during the testing. British servicemen, Australian soldiers and civilians were also exposed. The radioactive fallout caused sore eyes, skin rashes, diarrhoea, vomiting, fever, and the early death of entire families. The explosion caused blindness, and people suffered long-term illnesses such as cancer, blood and lung disease.'

'Shocking,' Paul said, his dark eyes on mine.

'Imagine that after fifty or sixty years you are finally allowed to return to your home, which has been used as an atomic test site. Even though it's declared safe, the land has changed. I watched a show where an Aboriginal woman said the land was bare, the trees and grass were all dead and there were probably no kangaroos.'

Paul concentrated on his breakfast.

'Imagine losing a sister in her twenties or an uncle in his forties to cancer; if it were me, I don't think I could forgive.'

'I doubt that any reasonable person could.' Paul shrugged. 'How long did the land remain contaminated and a health risk?'

'Who knows? It may still be,' I said.

'I get it,' said Paul. 'I do.'

'The injustice can't be healed; it extends through time and denies peace to the victims,' I said. 'Anyone who has been subjected to such injustice or who has suffered such trauma would struggle to feel at ease in the world; the horror is never extinguished. How do you regain your faith in humanity, which has already been damaged by generations of mistreatment, then destroyed by such injustice? That's the reality...' I was too upset to speak.

Paul drank his coffee. He seemed thoughtful. 'What about

land rights over the Maralinga land?'

'I think I'm right in saying that the South Australian government granted the Maralinga people title to the land in the early 80s, and in the early 2000s most of the Maralinga area was handed back to its traditional owners, having been declared "safe".' I added air quotes to the last word. 'Emu was returned in the 90s and, in 2014 I think it was, the federal government relinquished ownership of the weapons-testing range, the last parcel of traditional Aboriginal land to be returned.'

'I'm sure I read recently that the local people are setting up a tourism business to take visitors on bus tours through the test sites.'

'I don't think I'll be taking a tour in the foreseeable future,' I said in a hollow voice. 'Do you realise that the British knew in the 1960s that the radioactivity was worse than first thought? But they didn't tell the Australians.'

Paul looked at me in surprise. 'How do you know that?'

'I've known about it for years. There was an article back in the 90s I think, in *Scientific America* magazine.' I polished off the last of my bagel and continued. 'No one will ever know with certainty who in the British government knew about the radioactivity levels but what is certain is that those who knew and failed to divulge the truth committed a crime against Australian citizens.'

'If that's true, it's outrageous.'

'It's true all right, I have no doubt about that,' I countered.

'So, what are conditions like around the test sites now?'

'According to the authorities, the clean-up achieved the safety standards set at the start of the process.'

'Does that mean there's unrestricted access to those areas?'

'Yes, but as a precaution, there's an area of around 400

square kilometres where no one can live permanently.'

'Who paid for the clean-up?' Paul asked.

'In 1993, the Australian government and the traditional owners made representations to the British government.'

'And what did they achieve?'

'The Australian government received an ex gratia payment of £20 million towards the cost of rehabilitating the land.'

'Was that enough? What was the cost of the clean-up?' Paul leaned back in his chair and wiped his mouth with his napkin.

'It was over A$100 million.'

'So the British paid less than half!' Paul said, his voice hard. 'What about the Indigenous people? Did they get anything?'

'Well, it's not straightforward. A British legal firm had hoped to represent one hundred and fifty or so civilians if a class action by a thousand British veterans had succeeded. But the UK Supreme Court blocked the action, saying it would be impossible to prove radiation exposure was the cause of an illness sixty years after the event.'

Paul stared at me in disbelief. 'That's outrageous.'

I held up a hand. 'However, in 1991–92 the federal government made a payment of $618,000 to various Indigenous groups around Maralinga for land contamination. And in 1995, Aboriginal people received $13.5 million dollars from the British government for the loss of their lands. As compensation for the contamination, they then received another $6 million in 2009 when most of the Maralinga area was handed back to help them maintain the township.'

'And how much did they get as compensation for exposure to radiation?' Paul asked, his voice tight.

'To date only five people have been paid a total of $200,000 and claims by fourteen Aboriginal people have been rejected.'

* * *

After breakfast, I walked along the footpath to my car, where I sat for a long time thinking about Paul and our conversation. Why had he defended Menzies when I first mentioned that he should never have allowed Maralinga to be used by the British to test its nuclear weapons?

Driving home along Alexandra Avenue under the canopy of plane trees I was reminded of the differences between Paul and me. He had always been a conservative Liberal voter whereas I was a traditional Labor voter. I identified and sympathised with those less fortunate in society, whereas he respected and identified with people who lived in Toorak and drove fancy European cars. He often regarded people on social welfare as failures, many of whom, he believed, abused or took advantage of the system. I saw them as people in need.

At home, I threw the car keys in the bowl on the hall table and called out to Sara.

'I'm in the lounge room,' she said. 'How was breakfast?' She placed her book face down on the coffee table as I came into the room and I saw it was Bernhard Schlink's *The Reader*.

'Unsettling,' I muttered as I sat down.

'Why? What were you talking about?'

'I made the mistake of saying Menzies should never have allowed the British to use Maralinga to test their nuclear weapons.'

'And?'

'He got annoyed.'

'Oh, I'm sorry to hear that,' Sara said quietly.

'It really frustrates me that, as far as he's concerned, the Libs can do no wrong.'

'You always say that. Why do *you* get so upset?'

'Because he's like a horse with blinkers; he should consider every issue on its merits.'

'But the two of you have always seen the world differently,' she said, shaking her head.

'When you think of the damage the British did to our land, the dislocation of our Indigenous people, the destruction of their culture and the refusal of the British to take responsibility for the damage they caused, I can't see how anyone could try to justify what Menzies did.'

'All true,' Sara said. 'Did he try to justify it?'

'Yes, of course he did,' I said. 'At first...'

'And then?'

'Well, he softened a little in the end, I guess.'

'There you are, then.' She sat forward in her chair and said, 'Remember, our experiences colour the way we behave and the way we see the world. It may have taken Paul a little while to decide what he thought about the matter.'

Outside, it had started to rain. The branches of the street trees were soon dripping with water, and rain streaked the window; it was as if grey rain filled the world.

* * *

That night I dreamed I was back in Mr Kowalski's cellar. Our family had been one of the lucky ones. My father had got word that the Nazis were doing terrible things to the Jews. At any time of the day or night, helpless Jews were being dragged out of their homes. They were allowed to take only one piece of luggage and a bit of cash, and even then they were robbed of their possessions. Families were being torn apart; men, women and children were separated. Children came home from school to find their parents had disappeared. Women returned from shopping to find their home sealed, their families gone. Everyone was scared.

Mr Kowalski was an old school friend of my father's and

Papa arranged for us to escape to his farmhouse in the country where we remained for the duration of the war. Mr Kowalski and his wife risked their lives letting us stay in their cellar and bringing us any spare food. Had they been caught by the Nazis, they would have been shot for collaborating with Jews.

Our family spent 777 days in Mr Kowalski's cellar. I recall the monotonous rhythm of life down there. At 6.00 am I would hear Mr Kowalski's alarm go off. He'd get up, put the kettle on, and go to the bathroom. After thirty minutes, the bathroom would be free, and it would be Mama's turn. While Mama was in the bathroom, Dad would remove the blackout screen from the windows in the door. Then the rest of our family had a turn in the bathroom. The risky hour was 8.00 am, when the farmhands were starting to arrive. Any noise from us was dangerous because the farmhands were unaware of our existence. There was no doubt about our being killed if we were discovered. At 9.00 am, the farmhands started work in the fields, which were near the cellar. We walked around in socks and had to be quiet. The rest of the morning was devoted to reading and studying.

At 12.30 pm, the farmhands went home for lunch, and Mrs Kowalski came down to the cellar with our lunch. Mr Kowalski usually stayed upstairs to keep an eye out. It was nice for us to see other people and to hear the latest news from town. At 1.00 pm, the radio was switched on for the BBC Polish Service. They were risking their lives to have that radio, let alone listen to the BBC.

At 1.30 pm, the workers returned from lunch and resumed work. After Mama had cleared up the lunch things, she and Papa took an afternoon nap. I used that time for studying or writing in my diary. Around 4.00 pm, they had coffee, and then at 5.00 pm, the staff went home. Mrs Kowalski usually came down to see if we needed anything and we were no longer restricted to the cellar after that.

In the evening Papa wrote business letters on the typewriter, Mama did administrative chores and helped Mrs Kowalski cook dinner. After dinner, Mama and Papa read, talked, or listened to the radio. Around 9.00 pm, they started preparing for the night.

Every day when the sun went down, the windows in the door had to be blacked out. After that, the cellar fell silent. The next morning, the alarm would go off at 6.00 am again, and the monotonous routine of the previous day would be repeated.

Sundays were different. It was an ordeal to watch Mr and Mrs Kowalski pray for an hour. Then it was time to make the beds, scrub the floors and do the laundry. After a brief lunch break, during which we listened to the news, the cleaning and tidying up continued until about 2.00 pm. After another round of radio news, a music program and coffee, it was time for an extended siesta. Mama and Papa would go back to bed for a few hours. I never understood why my parents needed to sleep in the afternoon.

Sunday was the most miserable day of the week. If I was not required to help, I wandered from one room to the next while my parents did the cleaning, then down the stairs and back up again. Outside, the air was fresh, but in the afternoon, I lay down on the sofa and slept to shorten the time. The silence and the terrible fear of being caught were ever-present. Before dinner, we listened to a concert on the radio. After dinner and the dishes, I was relieved that another incredibly boring Sunday was over.

But no matter how bad the monotony, being sick was worse. I remember one time when I had a cold. With every cough, I had to duck under the blanket to avoid making a noise. Most of the time, the tickle refused to go away, so I had to drink milk with honey or suck cough drops. I still remember all the cures I was subjected too, sweating out a fever, steam treatments, wet compresses, dry compresses, heating pads and hot-water bottles.

After the war my father stayed in contact with Mr Kowalski and when Papa discovered he and his wife had fallen on hard times and were intending to sell their farm, Papa stepped in and sent them money each month to prop them up financially and enable them to stay on the farm. 'They saved our lives, it's the least I can do,' he would say to my mother.

* * *

Sara gave me a brief, tentative smile as she came in with a coffee for me.

'I think I can understand why Paul refuses to say Menzies was wrong,' I said, taking the coffee and smiling my thanks.

Sara glanced out the window. The rain had stopped, and the sun was breaking through the clouds.

'I think that Paul needs security and predictability to feel safe – look at the way he's lived his life, managed his career... For him, Menzies would have represented all the virtues.'

Sara smiled at me and said, 'I'm sure you're right.'

I sipped the coffee. It was excellent. 'But as far as I'm concerned,' I said, 'I think every Australian should feel ashamed about what Menzies allowed to happen at Maralinga.'

2

Nazi Collaborators

'What's wrong, Stephen?' Paul said as I sat down for breakfast at Darling Street Café, our regular breakfast place. It was a cold, overcast Saturday morning and the sun was hidden behind clouds, but there was a cheerful hum from people talking at surrounding tables.

'Why do you ask?'

'Because you look like you've seen a ghost; you're pale, your eyes are red…'

'Well, I slept badly last night. I was reading about the *kapos*, the *Sonderkommandos* and other Jews who collaborated with the Nazis inside the concentration camps.' My voice sounded rough and crackly.

To my surprise, Paul's eyes filled with tears. He looked away and said, almost under his breath, 'Unless you were there, you don't know what went on inside the camps and just how bad the *Sonderkommandos* were.' Then he coughed in that nervous way he does. He looked at me for a moment and said, 'Believe nothing of what you hear and only half of what you read.' Then he turned towards the window and fell silent.

'You're right,' I said as Bret, our waiter, arrived at the table.

'Your usual, gentlemen?' he said brightly.

We nodded and I went on. 'I've also been reading Primo

Levi – Sara bought it, but I got to it first; he was deported to Auschwitz in February 1944.' I could not keep the sadness from my voice.

Paul remained silent for a long time, just staring at me. Then he said, 'My friend Moshe told me a story some years ago.' He took a moment to order his thoughts. As I waited for him to continue, the chatter in the café seemed to grow louder. I turned to the two women at the next table and put my finger to my lips, asking them to lower their voices. They shrugged and smiled.

'Moshe told me that one Sunday morning there was a knock on the door and his wife opened it. He heard a man's muffled voice and then she called to him, "Fundraising". He went to fetch his wallet, and when he got to the door, he looked long and hard at the man collecting for the Blue Box. Moshe realised the man was a *Sonderkommando* at Auschwitz when Moshe was incarcerated there, and had been responsible for selecting Jews for the gas chamber. Moshe recalled the time when a prisoner was absent from roll call. He and all the other prisoners were made to stand in line for fifteen hours in the snow and rain. When the prisoner was eventually tracked down, he was tortured and then hanged. Moshe and the other prisoners were forced to watch. Seeing this man again, Moshe fainted – he just collapsed – and by the time he got to his feet the man had disappeared. He never saw him again.'

I clasped my hands together tightly to stop them trembling, trying to put myself in Moshe's shoes and grasp the magnitude of what Paul had said. I tried to imagine what it would be like to see a friend subjected to a public hanging, but couldn't. I felt disgust rise like bile and my stomach turned. I sat there a long time, feeling as if I were crying on the inside.

'It was the job of the *Sonderkommando* to run the crematoriums,' I said finally, my voice cracking on the last word, 'but I don't know how they could...'

Paul nodded slowly and said, 'Not just the crematoriums. They were the ones to decide who would be sent to the gas chambers. And it was their job to pull the corpses from the chambers, extract any gold teeth from jaws, sort clothing and transport the bodies to the crematoriums. They had to operate the ovens and dispose of the ashes.'

'What a shocking thing to have to do,' I said.

'Why do you say, "have to"?' Paul snapped.

'Because they were handpicked by the SS and if they refused they were shot on the spot.' I paused as Bret placed our coffees on the table, then I continued. 'The SS chose the *Sonderkommando* from among the Jewish prisoners based on their physical strength, facial features or in some cases as punishment—'

'But they were given extra food,' Paul interrupted. 'They got more than the average daily ration of 800 calories for their trouble.'

'I know it wasn't the 2000 calories a day needed to survive,' I said quietly, 'but you're being hard on them.' I couldn't keep a note of disapproval from my voice. 'I know from my reading that, every few months, each *Sonderkommando* squad was murdered by the SS. Then the next squad had the task of burning the corpses of their predecessors, to make sure they didn't survive to tell others what was happening.'

Paul said nothing, just gazed into his coffee.

'So, I wonder how the man who came collecting survived,' I said. I glanced at him and saw there was a strange, brooding grief in his eyes, which were sombre now behind his steel-rimmed glasses.

'Moshe said he had the man traced and discovered he was a well-known pathologist who worked closely with Mengele – the so-called Angel of Death – you know, the SS physician who conducted inhumane medical experiments on Jews and other "undesirables". Mengele gave this pathologist special treatment; that's how he became one of the few survivors of Auschwitz.' Paul seemed to be holding himself tightly, and his lips trembled when he spoke. 'It's a shame he wasn't murdered by the Nazis.'

'Don't be so quick to condemn him,' I said quietly. 'What would you have done if you were in his position? The Nazis eliminated anyone who refused to do their dirty work.'

'Yes, but he didn't object to working with Mengele.'

I sat there and listened in disbelief. 'You don't know that!'

Paul remained silent.

'Just think, every day they had to struggle to survive against the cold, hunger, beatings, fatigue, to cling to life for as long as possible at any cost... their feelings of powerlessness must have distorted their view of the world and led them to cooperate with the Nazis,' I said. 'The system is to blame.'

Paul sat upright. 'I disagree.'

'But what would any of us do when faced with the choice of either living or killing a fellow Jew? It's an interesting thought experiment,' I said.

'*Thought experiment*,' Paul snorted. I noticed his chin quivering.

'From what I've read, after liberation, no one spoke willingly about what had happened,' I said. 'Some of those who were complicit with the Nazis carried the guilt of what they had done. Others were able to console themselves in the belief that, if they had not done it, someone else would have.'

Paul buried his face in his hands, and sobs racked his

body. The two women sitting near us turned to look at him, then quickly turned away, not wanting to be seen gawping. I reached over to him and put my hand on his shoulder. He was trembling. After a long moment, he rubbed his eyes and sighed.

* * *

I couldn't get Paul and his account of Moshe's story out of my mind, and for once hardly noticed the roadworks and delays along Domain Road. Why had he been so hostile towards the man collecting for the Blue Box; so hostile that he wished him murdered by the Nazis? And why had Paul refused to sympathise with the dilemma faced by that man and the *Sonderkommandos*?

Memories of my childhood came flooding back. I recalled being puzzled by Paul's father's refusal to talk to me whenever I saw him. He was a tall, bald man, with no sense of humour. Mostly he was silent, withdrawn, his dark eyes lowered, as if lost in his thoughts. There was never any simple, intimate, human conversation between Paul and his father, and I had the impression they were incapable of communicating with each other about ordinary things. It troubled me, but I never mentioned it.

Paul's father would disappear into his study whenever I was invited to the house. At first, I thought he didn't like me, but Paul reassured me that he behaved in the same way with all his friends. There were times when, for no apparent reason, his temper got the better of him. One time, I remember seeing him standing at his desk in the study shouting into the telephone, his face pallid, his voice quivering, as he screwed a cigarette into the ashtray with a trembling hand. His anger was palpable, and I wondered what had prompted it. Conversely, there was a time when I had seen him at his desk weeping in silence. Why were Paul's family so concerned with leaving their past behind them when they arrived in Australia? And why did they refuse to look back?

***

I remember one time when we were still at school asking him if he had any siblings – it was early on in our friendship.

He shook his head, opened his mouth and then closed it. Finally he said, 'No.' For a long time he didn't speak, then eventually he said, 'Not anymore.'

'What does that mean?' I asked.

He gazed out the window at the new spring growth on the trees and muttered, 'What do you think it means, stupid? It means I had a twin brother, who died.'

'I'm sorry,' I said.

Paul was pale and seemed tense. I realised I should have kept quiet.

***

When I arrived home, Sara was standing at the window, waiting for me. 'How's Paul?' she asked.

'Not good,' I said. 'At breakfast, we were talking about the *Sonderkommandos* and he burst into tears.'

'Oh dear.'

'Then, driving home, I started to think about Paul and his father.'

'And?'

'Well, I thought about his father's anger.'

Sara nodded.

'I think when Paul's family escaped Europe and arrived in Australia, they were desperate to put the past behind them. It was as if they were trying to forget, or perhaps suppress something. Paul told me once his parents never spoke about the Holocaust, and they never spoke about his twin brother who died during the war. He said there was always this elephant in the room. That's how he was brought up.'

Sara was watching me closely. 'It's strange that the parents never spoke about their lost son.'

I considered her words, but before I could say anything she went on, 'I wonder how he died.'

I shrugged.

'I wonder if that was what turned the family off religion.' Sara hesitated and then said in a soft voice, 'Maybe something happened to Paul's brother during the war.'

* * *

The next Saturday, as I parked the car and walked towards the café, the sun broke through the clouds and cast long shadows on the footpath. I found Paul at our usual table sipping an orange juice.

Lifting his head from the paper, he looked at me with an uneasy grin. There was a long silence, and I wondered what he was thinking.

He faltered for a moment and said, 'Sorry if I was rude to you last week, but you touched a sore spot.'

Raising an eyebrow, I said, 'Really?'

Paul stared at me, then leaned forward and said, 'Sit down. I owe you an explanation.' His face was wan and there was a strange dead look in his eyes. His voice had a flat, toneless quality, almost as if someone else was talking through him.

'You remember my father, and how remote he was, or if not distant, then angry. I never understood it until one day I overheard him talking to my mother. It was a strange conversation, and at the time it made no sense to me. They were talking about the Warsaw Ghetto, the fighting, the loss of life. My mother was saying that he needed to move on. He needed to accept the reality that his family was lost. At the time, I was too young to realise what she was referring to. But now, when I reflect on that discussion, I suspect my father lost all his family in the uprising. He never spoke about his parents or about any siblings, and I was always too afraid to ask.'

'That's awful,' I said, remembering how I had disliked Paul's father.

'Did you ever wonder why Anna and I never had children?' he said, abruptly changing the subject. He took a deep, unsteady breath and continued. 'My family was deported to Auschwitz in 1944.' Then he added, 'I knew the man in Moshe's story.'

I stared at Paul for a long moment, not yet realising the significance of his words, which echoed shockingly inside my head.

He continued. 'My brother and I were separated from our parents on arrival.'

Outside, the wind blew through the branches on the street tree, sending the last few leaves tumbling.

'Three times a week my brother and I were locked naked in a room, for six to eight hours. Mengele injected us with God knows what. We were used as human guinea pigs, measured and studied...'

I stared at him, horrified.

'Fuck Mengele and fuck the Nazis.' A long, searing torrent of vile and hate-filled words poured out of him.

'Mengele took blood from one arm and gave us injections in the other. One time, my brother became very ill and was taken to hospital. If he had died, Mengele would have given me a lethal injection and done a double autopsy.'

Paul was in a trembling rage. Inside my head his words, *Fuck Mengele and fuck the Nazis*, repeated and repeated. I knew Mengele had escaped to South America and died in 1979, but this was not the time to mention it.

'Fortunately, my brother didn't die. But, undeterred, Mengele carried on experimenting with us and, as a result, my brother's kidneys stopped growing.'

Paul's voice became flat and toneless once more. He leaned forward, sighed and said, 'Auschwitz was finally liberated by the Soviet army on the 27th of January 1945. Eventually we were reunited with our parents and came to Australia.'

I sat there, unable to speak.

'My brother died on the ship,' he said. His voice was gentle. 'And I was left with heart and respiratory problems and unable to have children; that's when my parents turned their back on God.'

I swallowed hard.

In a thin and distant voice, Paul said, 'Some survivors have forgiven their tormentors and been able to relieve themselves of the pain they experienced; others, like my family, have carried the pain. Sometimes it feels like magma, building and building because it cannot break through and escape.'

3

Reaganomics

'The prime minister has been talking up the budget and carrying on about Reaganomics all week,' I said as our waiter arrived and stood ready to take our order.

'Why shouldn't he?' Paul said, sitting back in his chair with a frown. 'Tax cuts on business and high-income earners mean wealth trickles down to everyone.'

'Ha!' I snorted. 'Look at what's been happening in the States!' I realised two things simultaneously: Bret, our waiter, seemed impatient, and I should have kept quiet. 'Let's order,' I said.

Paul and I usually avoided talking politics. As far back as our university days, we'd had differing opinions on many social and political issues. Apart from our common interest in medicine and girls, I was absorbed in literature, economics and politics and he was interested in sport. While he was at the football on many Saturday afternoons, I was handing out leaflets and explaining with passionate conviction why Australia should not have troops in Vietnam. 'It's a civil war,' I'd insist, but he didn't agree. To him, ideology was all that mattered, but he'd told me once that he appreciated my courage in standing up for what I believed in, my determination to make changes for the better and my good intentions.

At university, we often sat in the cafeteria drinking coffee. Then I used to listen to every word he and others said, careful not to interrupt, waiting patiently to speak, never raising my voice, and never pretending to know better. But I'd changed.

'Tax cuts grow the economy and provide a larger tax base, so we're all better off,' Paul insisted, taking up where we'd left off.

'I disagree,' I said levelly.

'Reagan slashed the top tax rate and reduced corporate tax,' Paul continued.

'Yes, but he also increased government expenditure and tripled the federal debt,' I countered.

Paul looked at me, and for a long moment, neither of us spoke. Then, as if playing his ace, he said, 'Trickle-down economics helped end the 1980 recession.'

'That's never really been tested,' I said. 'In all probability it was government expenditure that ended the recession.'

Paul seemed lost for words. I knew that he usually accepted what I said because he believed I was well read. While he often disagreed with me, I knew he respected me. I hoped he would still feel the same after breakfast!

'But George W Bush successfully used trickle-down economic policy during the 2001 recession,' Paul persisted.

'It's just as likely that monetary policy, not tax cuts, caused that recovery.' I hesitated a moment and added, 'Trickle-down economics isn't about across-the-board tax cuts. It's about tax cuts for corporations and high-income earners, and on capital gains. It benefits the rich.'

'Those tax cuts help everyone eventually,' he replied, 'hence the term, *trickle-down*.'

'But under Reagan, income inequality got worse,' I replied. 'Instead of trickling down, prosperity trickled up.'

Paul snorted. I glanced towards the counter. I was growing

hungrier by the minute. 'Look, when the rich get richer, benefits do not trickle down. According to the IMF, increasing income to the poor and the middle-class increases growth. Whereas increasing income to the top 20 per cent of the population results in lower growth.' Why couldn't Paul see what was as plain as day to me?'

A hungry man is a grumpy man, and I could feel my temper shortening. Where was our food? He caught me looking and within minutes we had our breakfast.

'And our coffees?' Paul asked him.

'Coming right up, sir.'

I was nettled by my friend's opinions.

'Extra tax cuts for the wealthy boost economic growth because they encourage an expansion of their business interests,' Paul persisted, tucking into his eggs.

'Unfortunately, tax cuts to the wealthy do not translate into increased employment, consumer spending or increased government revenue; they simply increase inequality. Trump's tax cuts evidence this.' I promised myself I would say no more.

***

After breakfast, I breathed in the sharp autumn air as I walked the few blocks to my car. Driving home along St Kilda Road, bored and frustrated by the traffic, I thought about my breakfast conversation with Paul. I asked myself what it was about our upbringing that made us see the world so differently.

Paul had been born in Warsaw and had come to Australia in the mid-1950s, about the same time my family arrived from Lochow in Poland. But I had been born into a religious family, whereas Paul's family was not religious. As a young boy in Australia, I recall going to synagogue with my father on Shabbat. He would wear a long black coat and hat, and his greying beard reached down to his chest. He would nod to the bearded men in fur-trimmed hats as he entered, and always appeared comfortable in the noisy, jostling crowd inside the synagogue. To me, it seemed to be a place filled with religious fervour, enthusiasm and happiness, a place of noisy pleasure. The sound bounced off the walls of the synagogue, ecstatic, pulsing, as my father and I sat quietly, watching and listening, as I felt the joy of the Shabbat move through me. Now and then, a man standing on the *bema* banged his hand on the lectern and shouted, *'Quiet, quiet,'* and everyone in the synagogue was suddenly silent.

For the Shabbat dinner that followed my father usually invited a family less fortunate than us back to our home for a meal of soup with kreplach, chicken, and stewed apples for dessert. The evening was filled with prayers, singing and laughter, and the unspoken message that we should care for those less fortunate than ourselves.

I recall one evening, after our Shabbat meal, lying in bed thinking of my father and his welcoming and generous nature and realised how different my upbringing was from Paul's.

We had met at University High School; it was autumn then, too. While I was eating my lunch in the quadrangle, Paul had come over to my table, smiled shyly, sat down, and said he was having difficulty with his algebra, and asked me to give him a hand. From then on, we studied together, finished high school together, studied medicine and graduated together and then went into our separate specialities – Paul into ophthalmology, and I into paediatrics. But we have remained lifelong friends, despite our differences. Paul had built up a successful private practice in South Yarra, whereas I had done several stints overseas and with Aboriginal health services as a volunteer and had mainly worked at the Children's Hospital.

Paul came from a wealthy family who were deeply concerned with assimilating into Australian society and gaining wealth and financial security, and he had certainly managed to do that. His father built a large business in Flinders Lane in the city, making women's garments from fabrics he imported from Europe. He employed hundreds of machinists to make the skirts, dresses and blouses that he sold to Myer and other big retail outlets. I remember Paul telling me one time when we were sitting in the café at university that his father was a staunch Liberal voter because he believed their dry economic policies were good for employers. And when I asked whether his father cared about the machinists employed by him, Paul said dismissively, 'Dad says, "I'll feed my family and they can feed theirs."' I remember Paul quoting his father's logic with approval: 'And when Dad has to sack someone, he justifies it by saying, "It's the survival of the fittest. If one of us is going to go broke it's not going to be me, because if I go broke, none of them will have a job."'

There was a cruel indifference to Paul when he spoke, and I sometimes grew angry. Paul had insulated himself from the poor and the disadvantaged, and I don't think he understood how heartless his lack of sympathy was for those struggling to make a living. I had difficulty understanding his callous indifference. But that is how Paul had been brought up. It was very different from my upbringing, which had emphasised community, and care for our fellow human beings. Back then, when I listened to him speak, something inside me broke; I could feel it break.

Whenever I went to his place his father's refusal to talk to me puzzled me. It differed greatly from the way I had been brought up. At dinner, my father would ask what I had learned at school that day and we would discuss the Vietnam War, or

Martin Luther King and the civil rights movement or even the meaning of Bob Dylan's songs.

'He doesn't talk to me either,' Paul had said, 'except when he tells me to go to my room and study.' He'd continued, 'Some time ago I heard my mother ask him why he doesn't talk to me, and he said, "He doesn't need conversation, what he needs is study. He needs to get a good job and start earning a living. If that doesn't happen, I'll talk to him all right; and he won't like what I'll have to say."'

I grimaced. Poor Paul.

'I clearly remember standing in the hall listening to them argue,' Paul said, 'and when I entered the kitchen, Dad's face was ashen. He ground his cigarette into the ashtray and walked out. I don't know what they were arguing about, but he was furious.'

I'd sat on Paul's bed and listened as he talked on about his father. At last, his voice cracked, and he covered his face in his hands and wept. I went over and put my hand on his shoulder. I felt for his pain and for the years of his suffering, not knowing if his father loved him. He wept for a long time, and eventually I left him to collect himself and walked to the window. It was late in the afternoon and the setting sun cast a glow over the tall magnolia in the front yard. I turned and saw Paul wiping his eyes. He sighed, then said quietly, 'If nothing else, his silence has helped me become self-sufficient; it has given me strength.'

Remembering that boy from long ago, I felt mean for having lectured him on economics that morning.

***

When I arrived home, my wife Sara was in the front garden raking leaves. As I opened the car door, she smiled and said, 'How was your morning, Stephen?'

'Very thought-provoking,' I said, walking over to her. 'At breakfast, Paul and I got into an argument about Reaganomics. But then, driving home, I started to think about why Paul and I see the world so differently.'

Sara leaned the rake against a tree and followed me inside. I held the door open for her and said, 'I think when Paul's family escaped Europe and arrived in Australia, they were probably desperate to put the past behind them. They wanted to fit in, and in the process, they distanced themselves from religion. That's how Paul was brought up. Perhaps that resulted in a lack of empathy for others.'

There was a long silence, then Sara said, 'What's interesting is that your families escaped Europe, but you have dealt with the Holocaust so differently.'

I considered her words, but before I could answer she went on. 'You're much more compassionate to the plight of the underprivileged than Paul is.'

'Thanks.' I smiled self-consciously.

'And he's irreligious. Even before he met Anna at university, he seemed to rebel against religion; he didn't take it seriously.'

'But he likes the traditions of Judaism, even though he doesn't believe in creation or the existence of God,' I said.

'That's right, he regards religion as a bit of a joke, but he enjoys a Shabbat meal with Anna's family, and he celebrates Passover and the other festivals.'

'Yes,' I said. 'But I was never able to get him to come to synagogue with me on a Friday night.'

'You have always been a small-L liberal, more sympathetic to left-wing ideas. But Paul's quite naïve about what goes on in the real world.'

'That's why I married you,' I said, smiling. 'You have the emotional intelligence, insight and understanding I lack!'

***

The following Saturday I entered the café and found Paul at our usual table sipping a juice. Lifting his head from the newspaper, he fixed me with an uneasy look. A faint smile played around the corners of his mouth. This wasn't his usual warm greeting. The smile faded, and I wondered what he was thinking.

'I have a confession to make,' he said as I sat down.

Raising an eyebrow, I asked, 'What's that?'

'Before I go on, let me tell you what I saw on TV this week.'

I signalled to Bret, then indicated he should continue.

'There was a program about people living on the dole. Not unemployed people, but people like us… normal people, I mean.'

'*Normal* people?' I asked quizzically.

'People with jobs and normal lives, you know what I mean.'

'Okay,' I said, 'go on.'

'One of them was like me. I mean, I agreed with most of what he said, but then things got worse and worse for him. And to be honest, I couldn't see a solution any more than he could. He was stuck.'

Paul was staring down at his hands, his voice subdued. 'It was pretty grim.'

I waited for him to continue.

'I thought about what my father used to say, and what you've said for all these years…'

I suppressed a smile.

'I don't mean I'm turning into a bleeding heart,' he added gruffly, 'but it made me think.'

Bret brought us our coffees while Paul continued to talk. 'I think my views have softened a little. It's made me think about people like the ones on that show. Doing it tough. And how the government has been pretty harsh…'

I smiled and said, 'I agree with you.'

'It's made me think carefully about how my father was, about how I was brought up and how he shaped my views.' He took off his glasses and wiped them.

I didn't say anything, but I thought it was the perfect metaphor.

A faint smile played around the corners of his mouth again. 'And I've also checked up on what you said.'

'Oh?'

'Yes.' He sighed. 'You were right. Each time the government pursues a dry economic policy, the margin between rich and poor grows bigger, as you said.'

I stared at Paul for a long moment, understanding the significance of his words. Then he said, 'Funny how sometimes life teaches us things at exactly the right time.'

4

IBM and the Holocaust

'Sorry I'm late, but I was reading that book you gave me,' I said, as I sat down at the table, not realising Paul was in the middle of ordering his breakfast with a new waiter.

'Which book?' Paul asked, after I'd given my order, too.

I waited until I'd filled our water glasses and taken a sip from mine. 'The new edition of Edwin Black's book – *IBM and the Holocaust*. I got so immersed in it I couldn't put it down. I completely lost track of time.'

'Oh, good. Anna thought you'd find it interesting, that's why we got it for you.' He smiled.

'It is hard to believe, though, isn't it? Thomas Watson, the president of IBM, personally involved with Hitler's campaign to wipe out the Jews?'

Paul yawned hugely then said, 'Sorry, I've been having trouble sleeping, and to add insult to injury, when I do finally get to sleep, I have bad dreams.' He rubbed his eyes and said, 'Watson must have been so interested in profit that the destruction of the Jewish people was inconsequential.'

'I think that for Watson and the company it was never about anti-Semitism or National Socialism, it was only ever about money,' I said. 'They had no social conscience. All they cared about were profits for their shareholders.'

Paul blinked. He was looking at me, but didn't seem to be seeing me.

'*If it can be done, it should be done*,' I said, breaking the silence. 'That was the company mantra.'

'I must get round to reading it,' Paul said.

'You should,' I said. 'I think you'd be fascinated. You know, according to Black, Hitler used IBM punch cards to identify Jews, confiscate their assets, put them in ghettos and deport them to extermination camps.' I ticked off each of these on my fingers.

The waiter brought our coffees, and I paused until he left us, then continued. 'Yes, Black interested me, so I researched him. Did you know the first edition of his book – published in 2001 – was based on 20,000 documents drawn from archives in seven countries? It detailed IBM's twelve-year collaboration with Hitler.'

Paul nodded.

'It was initially published in forty countries, and what's more, IBM never denied any of the information in the book! And despite thousands of requests for a response, the company has always remained silent. Can you believe it?'

Paul began to cough. I stopped and watched helplessly as his thin frame bent and shook. Then he wiped his lips and eyes and nodded for me to continue.

'The new edition of the book, published in 2012,' I said, 'contains IBM correspondence, State and Justice Department memos, and concentration camp documents that detail the company's actions and what they knew during the Hitler regime.'

Paul was silent for a long time.

'You know they set up their Dutch subsidiary in 1941 to work with the Nazis?' I said. 'Well, all that correspondence was included in those 20,000 documents, along with Thomas Watson's approval for the 1939 release of special IBM alphabetising machines to help the Nazis rape Poland and deport their Jews.

'And the photos! There's one of the punch cards developed for the statistician who reported directly to Himmler and Eichmann.'

'Punch cards were the forerunner to the IBM computer,' Paul said, appalled.

I nodded. 'Initially, they were designed to track people. From the beginning of the Hitler regime in January 1933, IBM used its punch cards to accelerate Hitler's destruction of the Jews. At first, the cards were managed at IBM headquarters in New York, and later by its subsidiaries in Europe.'

I could hear my voice growing louder. 'Among the punch cards is one for the Race Office, which specialised in racial selections, and another card which was custom crafted for Richard Korherr, a Nazi statistician and expert in Jewish demographics who reported directly to Heinrich Himmler and worked with Adolf Eichmann. They were architects of the extermination of the Jews. The punch cards bear the indicia of IBM's German subsidiary.'

Outside, the rain had stopped.

Leaning forward with my forearms on the edge of the table, I said, 'Did you know that in 1937 Hitler gave an award to Watson to honour his exceptional service to the Third Reich? The medal, the Order of the German Eagle with Star, adorned with swastikas, was worn on a sash over the heart.' I stared at Paul, and we locked eyes for a moment. 'Watson returned the medal in June 1940 because of public outrage.'

'What a terrible man,' Paul said. 'The Talmud says that every man is responsible for what he does, because he has a will and by that will he directs his life.' His lips trembled with indignation. 'Even though I'm not religious, I agree with that!'

'The apologists have said the return of the medal shows that IBM and Watson had second thoughts about their alliance with Hitler and the Reich, but I doubt it frankly. There is a letter a year later, dated 10 June 1941, prepared by IBM's New York office, confirming that in 1940 IBM directed its Dutch subsidiary to set up a system for Hitler to identify and liquidate the Jews of Holland.' I could feel a pounding in my head, but I took a deep breath and continued. 'So, returning the medal was nothing more than a public-relations ploy.'

I could see Paul trembling slightly and realised I had probably been insensitive. 'Do you want to change the subject?' I asked in a quieter voice.

He gave me a long look, then shook his head, as if to say, *Continue*.

'Similar subsidiaries were set up in Poland, France, and elsewhere, in line with the Nazi takeover of Europe, and IBM maintained a site in most concentration camps and used punch cards to process, identify and track prisoners. They tattooed a number into the forearm of every Jew who entered the camp and numbered each camp.' As I bent to retrieve the book from my bag I noticed Paul unconsciously grip his forearm. I had seen the tattoo when we were children, but it had been removed a long time ago, leaving a faint scar. I flipped through the pages until I found the right page. 'For example, Auschwitz was coded 001, Buchenwald was 002; Dachau was 003, and so on. And prisoners were also numbered. Homosexuals were 3, 9 was for anti-social prisoners, and 12 was for Gypsies. IBM designated the number 8 for Jews. What's more, inmate deaths were similarly numbered: 3 represented deaths by natural causes, 4 by execution, 5 by suicide, and 6 represented those Jews who were sent to the gas chambers. Those bastards even had codes to differentiate between a Jew who had been worked to death and one who had been gassed.'

I felt my face grow hot.

'They printed the cards, configured the machines, trained the staff, and updated the system each fortnight on site in the concentration camps,' I said, outrage plain in my voice.

I looked at Paul then and noted the deep lines on his forehead. He had never been a happy person, but there had always been some moments when he had seemed more light-hearted. That was all gone now. Sara was right; I could see he carried the burden of his past. But I seemed unable to stop talking. My rage and frustration demanded expression.

'In the new edition of the book there are photographs that show the bunker at Dachau. It housed at least two dozen machines which were controlled by the SS. The bunker was constructed of reinforced concrete and steel and was designed to withstand the most intense aerial bombardment. IBM equipment was among the Reich's most important weapons...' I shook my head. 'Watson personally approved expenditures on bomb shelters and other installations because the cost was borne by the company, and he personally received a one per cent commission on all Nazi business profits.'

I flipped through the book again.

'I found two US government memos amazing. The first is a State Department memo that was written on the 3rd of December 1941, four days before the attack on Pearl Harbor. The Nazis were being accused of genocide in Europe and IBM's attorney, Harrison Chauncey, visited the State Department to express his fear that IBM might be accused of cooperating with the Nazis.'

Paul leaned forward and shook his head. 'With good reason,' he said. 'They did collaborate.'

'And there was a second astonishing memo. It was from the Justice Department. During a federal investigation into IBM, the chief investigator, Howard Carter, prepared a memo describing the company's collusion with Hitler's regime.' I scanned the page and paraphrased: 'He claimed there was no real difference between IBM and the Nazis in terms of the damage they were doing.'

Paul fixed his dark eyes on me. I glanced out the window and thought fleetingly that the sky seemed to be crying. The breeze had picked up, tossing the fallen leaves on the pavement.

'You know, the Treaty on Genocide defines genocide as any act intended to destroy a racial or religious group, and it states that complicity in genocide is a punishable offence,' Paul said. 'Clearly Thomas Watson and IBM were guilty of genocide.'

'Paul,' I said, 'it worries me that future generations will tire of hearing about the Holocaust, that they'll grow weary and through the generations forget or stop accepting that it happened. Out of fatigue or ignorance the horror of the extermination camps will fade. Today, those who survived the camps can bear witness but, in the future, each of us has an obligation to never forget.'

He nodded, and then the waiter brought our breakfast, and we ate in silence.

***

After breakfast, I quickly ran to my car in the drizzle. I sat for a moment. Paul had seemed deeply shaken by our conversation. Driving home, I was acutely aware that, although we usually saw the world very differently, today we were in agreement.

When I arrived home, Sara was in the kitchen, sitting at the table eating cereal with fruit and yoghurt.

'Good morning,' she said, dipping her spoon into the bowl.

'You're off to a late start – did you sleep in?'

'I was reading in bed on my kindle.'

'What were you reading?'

'*Gilead*.'

'I don't think I know it.'

'It's a novel written by Marilynne Robinson. It's beautifully written.'

'What's it about?'

'Oh, it's about a Congregationalist minister in Iowa – Reverend John Ames – who sets down the story of his life for his son.'

'Is it interesting?'

'Yes, you should read it,' she said with a slight smile. 'I'm sure you'll enjoy it. Now tell me, how's Paul?'

'Hard to tell,' I said. 'You know that book he gave me, about IBM and the Holocaust? Well, I don't think he'd read it. He got pretty upset when I talked about it.'

Sara looked at me quizzically and asked, 'Did you ask him why?'

'No,' I said, shaking my head. 'But I felt very uncomfortable. I did ask him if he wanted to change the subject, but he said he didn't.'

'Hmm,' Sara said, then went on quietly, 'I'm embarrassed to say I don't know anything about IBM; what happened?'

'When Hitler came to power in 1933, computers didn't exist, obviously. But the IBM punch-card system did. It was the forerunner to today's computers. You'd have used punch cards at school, I'm sure. Anyway, that system was the one Hitler used to identify and target Jews, confiscate their assets, round them up and ship them off to the death camps for extermination.' Feeling the blood rise in my face and head, I stopped for a moment to take a breath. 'And then the system automatically catalogued Jewish remains.'

'So that's how the Nazis could get their victims to the camps so efficiently.'

'Yes.'

'It must have added to the Nazis' natural efficiency,' Sara said bitterly.

'And what's more, IBM used its own staff and equipment, designed, executed, and dispatched more than two thousand machines throughout Germany, and thousands more throughout Europe and each concentration camp. The company custom-designed the applications and trained the Nazis in the use of the cards and machines. IBM's top management comprised many Nazi sympathisers who courted Hitler from 1933.'

Sara's shoulders stiffened. She said, 'I always wondered how the SS were able to round everyone up so efficiently. They'd post a notice demanding those listed assemble at the train station for deportation, but where did those lists come from?'

'Well, now we know,' I said. 'They generated their lists using the IBM punch-card system.'

Sara's face showed her disgust and anger.

'It wasn't until I read Edwin Black's book that I realised that when IBM formed its alliance with the Nazis, it perfected the racial census that listed not just religious links, but bloodlines back through the generations. This was the information used by the Nazis to identify and count the Jews and so-called half Jews.' I took a deep breath to steady myself. 'Food allocation was also organised with the use of this database, allowing Germany to starve the Jews. Slave labour was identified, tracked, and managed through the punch-card system. And the cards made trains run on time and catalogued their human cargo. Punch-card installations were maintained at train depots across Germany, and across Europe.'

'I wonder how much IBM's head office in New York knew about this outrage?' Sara said.

'Plenty! I have no doubt that they knew. Although, I suspect they preferred to maintain the pretence of ignorance.'

Sara pushed her bowl to one side. 'How can you be so sure?'

In a tight voice I said, 'Watson's personal representatives, Harrison Chauncey and Werner Lier, were regularly in Berlin ensuring that head office was not cut out of any of the profits or business opportunities. And when US law made direct contact with the Nazis illegal, IBM's Swiss office became the conduit, providing the New York office not only with information, but credible deniability.'

She looked at me and frowned. 'This means a lot to you, doesn't it?'

'It does,' I said. 'You know how close I was to Dad's brother Herschel and his wife Ruth. Well Ruth escaped from a boxcar en route to Treblinka – I'm sure I've told you – was shot, and then buried alive in a shallow mass grave. Herschel had already run away from a guarded line of Jews and discovered her leg protruding from the snow – remember? By some miracle they survived, despite the cold, the hunger, and the Reich. So, when Paul gave me the book, reading it was a way of honouring them, and all the others. And I'm very interested in it. I suspected that IBM was somehow involved in the murder of those millions of Jews. There were bits of information everywhere and they just needed to be connected.'

Sara was quiet for a moment. 'What do you know about this Black, the author?'

'In 1998, he began his quest for answers. He recruited a team of researchers and translators and developed a network throughout the United States and Europe. Holocaust survivors, children of survivors, and students, as well as professional researchers, archivists and historians, and even former Nuremberg Trial investigators, began a search for documentation. More than one hundred people participated, some for months at a time and some for just a few hours.'

'Amazing,' she said.

I pulled the book out and scanned a few pages then began to read and paraphrase. 'Eventually, he amassed more than 20,000 pages from fifty archived documents located in library collections, museum files, and other sources. He retrieved thousands of previously classified State Department papers and hidden documents from Europe. He translated more than fifty books and memoirs, as well as professional and scientific journals including punch cards, Nazi publications, and newspapers of the era.'

Sara sat upright. 'Seriously impressive,' she said.

I continued. 'It was very clever. Many of the documents, viewed in isolation, said very little, but linked to other documents, they told a powerful story. It was like a jigsaw puzzle. The overall meaning couldn't be revealed until all the pieces were combined. The picture could only be constructed when all the fragments were put together.'

'He's to be applauded,' Sara said.

'Every private, public, and governmental institution in every country cooperated. Initially, and not surprisingly, the only refusal came from IBM. Since the Second World War, almost every book on IBM includes a reference to the company's refusal to cooperate, but somehow Black wore them down and eventually he gained access to a great deal of IBM documentation.'

Sara sat still, shaking her head in disbelief.

'He then gathered together a team of researchers and archivists to go through his book to make sure that every statement could be corroborated.'

'All very interesting. But you were telling me about Paul. Why don't you ask him about his reaction? You know him well enough. If he doesn't want to talk about it, he'll tell you.'

* * *

The following Saturday was overcast. I arrived at the café and found Paul at our usual table reading the paper.

As I sat down, Paul said, 'Uh oh. What's on your mind today? I know that look of yours.'

'I have a question for you.'

'What's that?' he said, lifting his chin.

'Last week, when we were talking about IBM and the Holocaust, you seemed very upset by our conversation.'

'And?'

'And I was wondering what it was that made you so upset?'

Paul removed his glasses, wiped his brow with the back of his hand, and said in a soft voice, 'I told you that my twin brother and I ended up with Mengele in Auschwitz; what I didn't tell you is that we had a little sister.'

He looked at me and I saw him force the corners of his mouth into a brief, sad smile, then he looked away. When he looked back at me, we locked eyes for a long, silent moment. His face was pale, the olive skin flat and lifeless. Shocked, I didn't know what to say.

Eventually, he continued. 'When we arrived at Auschwitz our family was separated on the platform. Our little sister Judy was taken for slave labour. My mother and father were sent off to one side and my brother and I to the other. I remember I held on to my brother for fear that we might be separated. But we soon realised that would not happen; we were to be used by Mengele for experimentation.'

Outside, the sky was oppressive, shrouded by thick clouds, and an icy wind blew in whenever someone opened the door.

Paul took a deep breath, swallowed, and continued. 'At first, my brother and I were stationed near Gas Chamber Number Four.' He hesitated for a moment. 'We saw unsuspecting women and children entering the gate to the gas chamber; they would have died within half an hour. At that time, the Nazis had the gas chambers going day and night.' Paul looked tired to the point of exhaustion.

'You don't have to continue,' I said quietly. I felt cold telling him that, but I didn't know what else to say.

He looked up and said, 'No, no. I should have told you this story long ago.'

But I could see from the brooding look in his eyes and the set of his face that it was difficult for him to talk about his sister. 'Are you sure?' I persisted. My words sounded lame.

He looked at me thoughtfully for a moment and said, 'After Mengele was done with us, my brother and I were sent to a forced labour camp in the Birkenau section of Auschwitz. Somehow, we managed to stay together. Sometime later we ran into our mother's younger sister, our Aunty Anne, who was in her late twenties. It was like finding a parent. She was such a huge emotional support for us.'

I could see he was struggling.

'When the Soviet troops approached in January 1945 the SS began the final evacuation of prisoners from Auschwitz. They marched thousands of Jews on foot, in rags, through the snow towards the interior of the German Reich.' His long, gaunt face seemed to have taken on additional lines.

'It must have felt as if the cruelty would never end,' I said, searching for sympathetic words.

'The SS guards shot anyone who fell behind from exhaustion.

Jews suffered from starvation, the cold, and exposure on those marches and more than 3000 died on route to Gliwice. Sadly, my Aunty Anne was one of them. She had become ill, and they murdered her.'

'I read somewhere that more than 15,000 died during the death marches from Auschwitz,' I said sombrely.

He turned and peered out the window, then closed his eyes, inclined his head, and seemed to be thinking. He said, 'In the confusion of the evacuation, we escaped and sheltered in an empty farmhouse nearby. The Soviets came but for some reason left again immediately, so we had to fend for ourselves.'

'You were lucky to escape the death marches,' I said.

Paul looked at me intently. 'Then, we spent months trying to get out of Poland, but first we returned to Warsaw in the hope of finding Judy. We had no idea what had happened to her and the rest of the family. Eventually, we were reunited with our parents, but there was no trace of our sister. Lists of those who were still alive were put up on buildings. We asked everyone we met, and every conversation was dominated by trying to find out where our little sister and other relatives were.'

I sat rigidly in my seat and said nothing. It wasn't long before Paul broke the silence and said, 'Unbeknown to us, Nazi soldiers took photos of the deportation of Polish Jews from the moment we got off the train at Auschwitz; they showed us going into the bath house and getting our prison clothes.'

My heart sank.

'These photos were discovered thirty years ago and despite their age, they completely captured the entire experience as I remembered it. We were dumbfounded, having had no idea they existed.' Paul paused for a moment. He tilted his head to look at me. His eyes were very dark.

'As it turned out, we ended up in a picture at the very

moment they separated us from Judy. It captured us standing on the platform at Auschwitz. My mother is leaning forward with tears in her eyes, trying to see our sister. Mama spent hundreds of hours scouring the photos with a magnifying glass, trying to find her daughter.'

I stared at him.

'In one of the photos she discovered her parents waiting in line for the gas chamber, but there was no sign of Judy.'

'That's terrible. What a story. So sad.'

'Now you know why I got so upset during our conversation; it reminded me of my sister.'

'When you arrived in Australia, did you contact the Red Cross?'

'Yes, like other Jewish families who had lost family members in Europe, we hoped they might have had word of what had happened to Judy. We never found her.' Paul's voice was tinged with anger, perhaps due to his sense of helplessness.

'Were they able to tell you anything?' I asked, noticing the deep frown lines between his eyebrows.

'They discovered she had been hidden in a cellar by a local couple who took pity on her.'

'But how—'

Paul held up a hand. 'Apparently, she escaped from the labour camp and was taken in by a couple, a Mr and Mrs Kruger, who hid her in their cellar. Mr Kruger was aware that the Nazis were going from house to house searching for Jews. So, they decided to pass her off as their own daughter. They assumed the Nazis would have no idea whether they had a child or not.'

'So far, so good,' I said cautiously.

Paul snorted.

'They had a list of everyone in the village. All the names,

race, religion, everything.' Paul's lips quivered.

'Oh no,' I said.

'Yes.' Paul's raspy voice pierced the silence in our corner of the café. He hesitated a moment to wipe his eyes with the back of his hand, and then continued. 'Now we know how that list was compiled.'

'And, and then what…?'

'That's it,' he said bitterly, 'that's all we were able to find out. The Nazis' impeccable record-keeping failed, but too late to save Judy.'

5

The House Un-American Activities Committee

'Are you now or have you ever been a member of the Communist Party?' I said to Paul as we walked in the door of the Darling Street café for breakfast. I nodded to our usual waiter and indicted our table.

'Do you have to ask?' he said dryly. 'I'm a surgeon, and a card-carrying member of the Liberal Party.'

I chuckled.

'Where's this coming from?' he added as he pulled back his chair and sat down. 'What have you been reading this time?'

'Charlie Chaplin's autobiography, and it's very interesting,' I replied. 'That was the question asked by the House Un-American Activities Committee.'

Paul hesitated a moment and then said, 'That was in the 50s, wasn't it?'

'That's right. It was set up in 1938, but its main activities were in the 50s.'

'Chaplin was a comic genius. It's a shame he was a communist sympathiser,' said Paul.

I wasn't certain, but judging by his slight smile, I suspected he might be trying to bait me.

'No, he wasn't,' I insisted. 'He was a liberal thinker, and

that was the extent of it.'

He shrugged, and I saw that he'd been serious. I remembered the many arguments we'd had at this table, and I realised we were probably in for another disagreement. I promised myself I would remain calm and considered in my responses.

'He and many others were victims,' I continued.

'Victims, my arse.' He gave me a straight look. 'Each and every one of them was a threat to our national security.'

'*Our* national security?'

'"The enemy of my friend is my enemy", isn't that how the saying goes?'

'I don't think so… but anyway, lots of Hollywood artists were unfairly blacklisted. And Charlie Chaplin was at the top of the list.'

'He was a parlour Bolshevik, a communist sympathiser…'

'Well, you and the FBI certainly agree on that. They thought he was a security risk, even though Chaplin denied all of it. FBI Director J Edgar Hoover wanted him deported and had MI5 spy on him when he was in London.'

Paul shifted on his seat, but he didn't reply.

I hesitated a moment and said, 'MI5 decided he wasn't a security risk; they said he was nothing more than a left-leaning progressive.'

Paul's eyes, clear and dark, locked with mine, and for a moment I felt his conviction. 'Nevertheless, Chaplin was banned from the US, wasn't he? And instead of fighting to re-enter the country, he decided to make his home in Switzerland. The fact that he didn't fight for his rights tells me he knew he was guilty.'

'That's simply not true. Chaplin said he was subjected to lies and propaganda by reactionary groups and it was impossible for him to continue working in the US, and that's why he gave up his US residency...'

'But,' Paul said, 'there were others as well, apart from Chaplin.'

I was silent a moment, shaking my head. 'Yes, that's true. Orson Wells was at the height of his career when the US government began investigating him; they had him on a short list of people who should be apprehended in case of a national emergency.'

Paul opened his mouth to say something, then turned away. He seemed lost for words.

'He knew he was being targeted by the FBI,' I continued. 'So, he left the country in 1948 and moved to Europe, where he lived for the next eight years.'

'Well, what about Leonard Bernstein? He was definitely a communist sympathiser.' Paul delivered this deadpan, so I wasn't sure if he was serious.

'He was against US involvement in Vietnam and supported the activities of the Black Panthers, so according to the FBI, he must be a communist!' I leaned forward in my chair and said in a deliberate voice, 'Even though he swore an affidavit saying he had never been a member of the Communist Party, the FBI spied on him for three decades and had him blacklisted at CBS.'

Paul smiled slightly, then he took a gulp of his coffee, placed it on the table and said quietly, 'All right, get it all off your chest. Who else? I know I won't have any peace until we've dealt with this latest bee in your bonnet.'

I hesitated, feeling slightly offended, but he waved me on.

'All right. Well, singer Lena Horne, screenwriter Dalton Trumbo, poet Dorothy Parker and many more were also targeted and blacklisted by the FBI. It meant they had difficulty finding work—'

'They got their just deserts. You forget the times, Stephen. Communism was on the march.'

Irritated by Paul's single-minded support of the US government I snapped, 'Why are you so keen on the US? Don't you realise that American eugenics laws were the blueprint for Germany's anti-Semitism?'

'That's hard to believe,' he said.

'Look, the Nazis' extermination program was carried out in the name of eugenics and American eugenicists laid the foundation for the program.'

He looked at me, still sceptical but beginning to waver. He knew I always checked my facts.

I persisted. 'Hitler boasted to his friends how closely he followed American eugenic legislation.'

Paul covered his mouth, dragging his hand down over his chin as he thought for a moment then asked, 'How do you know that?'

I looked straight at him and said, 'You can check for yourself. American states passed sterilisation laws based on eugenics in the early years of the twentieth century. Hitler argued that it was necessary to prevent severely handicapped people from living because it would lead to the improvement of everyone's health. And you know where that led.'

Anger flared in his eyes.

I sighed and looked out the window. Rain streaked the glass and filled the street with dismal mist. The bleak sky hovered low over the buildings opposite. *What's the point of trying to talk to Paul?* I thought. *What's the point of explaining to him that his admiration for conservative Americans is built on a false premise? Did I need to explain to him that after the war America sheltered Nazi sympathisers, not communists?*

'Do you know the background to the Committee?' I asked,

searching for safer ground.

'It was set up to investigate allegations of communist activity in the US during the early years of the Cold War, wasn't it?' Paul said.

'That's right. There were various earlier committees, and one was set up in 1938, but it became a standing committee after the Second World War, when tensions between the US and the Soviets intensified. 'That's when the committee escalated its investigations into communist activities in the US. And from 1947 onwards, it conducted a series of public hearings alleging that communists had infiltrated governments, schools, the entertainment industry, and many other areas of American life.'

Paul nodded slowly, but was silent.

I felt a heaviness in my chest, but I took a deep breath and persisted. 'The committee had power to subpoena citizens to appear in public hearings before Congress – it intimidated witnesses and, as a result, their revelations were questionable.' I took a sip of my coffee, then continued. 'The committee's tactics contributed to the fear and distrust and uncertainty that existed during the anti-communist hysteria of the 1950s.'

Paul shook his head. Undeterred, I persisted. 'The committee grilled individuals about their political beliefs and insisted they provide the names of other people who had taken part in allegedly subversive activities.'

'So, what else could they—'

Before he could finish, I said, 'Individuals who refused to answer questions or provide names were branded *red* and indicted for contempt of Congress, and some of them ended up in jail. Others who pleaded the Fifth created the impression that they were guilty, and so many were disinclined to do so. And those who refused to cooperate with the committee were often blacklisted; some lost their jobs and were prevented from working in their chosen industry.' I was filled with indignation once more and felt anger building inside me.

'The tactics used by the committee trampled on citizens' rights and ruined their careers and reputations,' I said. As I hesitated to collect my thoughts, Bret came up with our breakfasts, and for a while neither of us spoke. Then I said, 'Most people who were called before the committee had broken no laws but were targeted for their political beliefs or for exercising their right to free speech.'

Paul sighed and said, 'Given the grave threat to US security posed by communism, I think the committee was justified in what they did and how they went about it.'

'Oh, for heaven's sake. As I said earlier, they paid special attention to the motion-picture industry!'

He sighed. 'That's right. One of the most powerful propaganda machines in the world! I wish I knew what to say to convince you,' he said.

Ignoring his comment, I said, 'Did you know most film-industry executives did not complain? They feared losing the movie-going public and didn't want to get on the wrong side of Congress. Many of the major studios imposed a strict blacklist policy against actors, directors, writers and other personal implicated in "communist" activity.' I put air quotes around 'communist'.

Paul put down his knife and fork and said, 'I remember reading recently about a guy called Whittaker Chambers—'

'He was a self-confessed former member of the American Communist Party,' I said, interrupting Paul. He appeared before the committee in 1948. During his testimony, he accused Alger Hiss, a former high-ranking State Department official, of serving as a spy for the Soviet Union. Based on Chambers' evidence and allegations, Hiss was found guilty of perjury and spent several years in prison.'

'That's right.' Paul looked pleased with himself, like a boxer who has landed a winning blow.

'But don't forget that Hiss spent the rest of his life proclaiming his innocence and criticising his wrongful prosecution.'

'I don't care what you say, the committee uncovered vital information that bolstered national security, and the Hiss conviction is evidence of it,' Paul insisted, clearly fed up with the argument.

I shook my head sadly. 'I don't buy it. I suspect the committee was little more than a partisan tool to discredit the New Deal programs of President Roosevelt.' I chewed thoughtfully, then said, 'Did you know that Nixon was one of the members of the committee in the late 1940s?'

Paul looked at me and rubbed the side of his face. 'I don't understand you. There are many things in this world I don't understand, but you are the biggest mystery of all,' he said.

'What's there to understand? There's nothing wrong with having a difference of opinion. We see the world differently, that's all.'

He shrugged.

'Anyway, McCarthy's reign of terror ended in 1954, when the news media revealed his unethical tactics, and he was censured by his colleagues in Congress. And by the late 1950s and early 1960s, the committee's relevance was in decline. Then, in 1969, it was renamed the Committee on Internal Security. Finally, it ceased operations in 1975.'

'Shame there's not a degree in McCarthyism,' Paul said drily. 'You'd get a high distinction.'

'What is interesting,' I persisted, 'is that during that period, the line between civil liberties and national security became blurred. Some people felt their personal freedoms were being taken away, others believed the work of the committee was important for national security.'

Paul smiled. 'If nothing else, perhaps we can agree on that.'

* * *

After breakfast, I ordered another coffee and sat on at our table for a long time after Paul left. I couldn't get our conversation out of my mind. Why was he so preoccupied by national security and so quick to ignore the hard-fought gains and personal freedoms the Allies had battled so fiercely to preserve? And why did he see communism as a threat to national security? After all, it was Hitler and his fascist regime, not the communists, who persecuted the Jews.

Of course, Paul was an arch conservative and he and I seldom agreed. But I could see by his irritable reactions that there was no way I could convince him that the activities of McCarthy and his committee were nothing more than a political witch-hunt.

* * *

When I arrived home, I dumped my keys on the hall table and went through to the living room, where I could hear Sara talking to someone.

'You're late,' she said. 'Anna's been here for ages.'

I was surprised to see Paul's wife Anna sitting opposite Sara, a coffee cup balanced on her knee.

'Hello Anna,' I said, struggling to shake off my mood.

She smiled. 'How was Paul? How did he seem to you?' she asked.

'We were talking about McCarthy and the House Un-American Activities Committee, but we didn't see eye to eye, unsurprisingly.'

'So, what's new?' said Sara. 'You usually disagree.'

Anna glanced at her.

'No matter what I said, I could not convince him that the committee was abhorrent and an incursion on our civil liberties. He thought the activities of the committee were justified.'

'Is that so remarkable?' Sara asked.

'Well, given what he experienced under Hitler, I would have thought it would be the opposite, wouldn't you, Anna?'

She shrugged. 'Who knows?' she said. 'I sometimes feel I hardly know him at all.'

There was a long silence, then Anna said, 'I'd better go. I just wondered...' She looked down at her hands for a moment but didn't continue. 'Thanks for the coffee, Sara. Maybe we should meet up on Saturdays like Paul and Stephen.' She laughed and got to her feet.

Sara smiled and followed her out into the hall.

* * *

'Why was Anna here?' I asked when she returned.

'She's worried about Paul,' Sara said.

'So am I,' I said. 'He'll soon be further right than Genghis Khan.'

Sara sighed. 'Stephen, she's *really* worried about him.'

'Why?' I asked. 'He seemed fine to me. He had no problems arguing the merits of Joe McCarthy and the House Un-American Activities Committee.'

'I'm not sure about that, from what Anna was saying.' She hesitated a long moment then said, 'I have no doubt that Paul's Holocaust experiences have made him less sympathetic to others; he has learned through bitter experience to put himself first.'

'Perhaps. But then why support a regime that was seeking

to curtail individual liberties?'

'Who knows?' she said.

'If you consider what Paul went through in Auschwitz, I think he'd have a dislike for all totalitarian regimes, both communist and fascist, and yet he was cheering on McCarthy and sneering at Charlie Chaplin!'

'I've just finished reading a book you'd find interesting,' Sara said, if you want ammunition against the Americans. 'It's by Eric Lichtblau, *The Nazis Next Door.* He says thousands of Nazis settled in the United States after the Second World War. US intelligence was happy to assist them because they saw them as potential spies in the Cold War against the Soviets.' She ran a hand through her hair and continued. 'Lichtblau says there was a network of Nazis who spied for the US in Europe, Latin America and the Middle East after the war; they were rewarded for their service by being allowed to come and live in the United States.' She spoke quietly, but I could hear the pain in her voice.

'So, what are you telling me?' I asked, rubbing my forehead. 'Are you saying the US was more sympathetic to the fascists than the communists?'

'Yes. That was the position of the US government and the American people. If Paul were American, he'd be a patriot – as far as he's concerned, the Republicans can do no wrong. So, it's not surprising that he agreed that US security is more threatened by the Soviets than the fascists. I imagine he'd have no idea about anything that Lichtblau has uncovered.'

'What really concerns me is that Paul's rants ignore all that is good about America – I doubt that he realises that the more we move to the right, the closer we come to totalitarianism.'

Outside, the rain had eased. The gutters were no longer flooded with rushing streams of water.

'Did the average American know that there were Nazis living in the US?' I asked. I was intrigued by what Sara had told me.

She collected the two coffee cups and stacked them. 'Operation Paperclip was a secret US Intelligence Program that brought 1600 German scientists and engineers to the US for government employment between 1945 and 1959, but it wasn't until the late 70s that the media exposed them,' she said.

'Remember our conversation about IBM and the holocaust?'

'Yes, what about it?'

'America has blood on its hands when it comes to the Nazis – and their witch-hunt against the communists parallels the Nazi attitude to communists.'

'Yes, I can see how you could argue that. But you should read Lichtblau. It wasn't until 1979 that a Nazi-hunting unit was set up by Congress at the Justice Department – lawyers and historians began probing hundreds of alleged Nazis, Nazi spies and war criminals who were living throughout America.' Her dark eyes narrowed. 'According to Lichtblau, that was when the CIA cleansed their records. They must have realised that many of the Nazis had committed atrocities and so they removed Nazi material from their files.'

'This book sounds very interesting, tell me again who wrote it?'

'Eric Lichtblau, he's an investigative reporter for *The New York Times*. He won a Pulitzer with another guy for their stories on the National Security Agency's secret surveillance of American citizens.'

'I'll look forward to reading it when you've finished with it.'

'I've finished it. You can take it, I'm sure you'll find it fascinating, and you might even be able to convince Paul to read it.' Then she added, 'After liberation, there were thousands of Jews in displaced persons camps. They were kept under armed guard behind barbed wire, and they were bunked in with

Nazi prisoners. There were insufficient medicos and so Jews were treated by Nazi doctors and nurses. Thousands of them died of disease and malnutrition.' Sara shuddered. 'Disease was rampant – to kill the lice, they had to burn the buildings where prisoners had been kept. Lichtblau says, as easy as it was for the Nazis to get into America, it was very difficult for Jews to get out of the camps.'

'That's disgusting; it's offensive,' I said. 'No wonder they kept it from their citizens.' I felt anger surge through me. I wanted to kill every person responsible for letting Nazis into America. It was an outrage. 'To think that they could harbour such criminals demeans us all,' I said.

'It took Jews many months, and in some cases many years, to get out of those displaced-person camps,' Sara said in a thin, tight voice.

I felt the blood pounding in my head.

'General George Patton believed that the Nazis were best suited to run these camps and openly defied orders from General Dwight Eisenhower, who oversaw the European forces after the war.' She was talking quietly but with intensity. 'And don't forget, the British were also responsible for stopping Jewish refugees escaping Europe.'

I pulled out a chair and slumped into it, resting my head in my hands.

'Patton oversaw these displaced persons' camps. He allowed the Nazis to lord it over the Jews,' she said. She adjusted her glasses and continued. 'Just after the war there were very few immigration visas to get into the United States. There were thousands of senior Nazi officers and Nazi collaborators who, with the help of US intelligence, were able to obtain visas while the Jewish survivors could not.'

I shook my head slowly and felt something like despair.

'Some of them had been responsible for running Nazi concentration camps,' Sara said. 'Others had been the warden at a camp, or the secret police chief in Lithuania who signed the death warrants for people.' She took a deep breath. 'And what's worse, there were policymakers in Washington who said the Jews should not be let in because they were *lazy* or *entitled*.'

I raised my eyes to the ceiling, but Sara wasn't finished.

'The CIA, FBI, military and other US intelligence agencies recruited more than a thousand Nazis and Nazi collaborators after the war. They operated in Europe and inside the United States, Latin America, the Middle East, and even here in Australia.'

'Was this US government policy?'

'No, it grew organically from the network of Nazi spies in Europe, the Middle East and Latin America. After the war they came to the United States, one by one.' Sara was silent a moment, then she said soberly, 'As if all this isn't bad enough, according to Lichtblau there are documents that still remain classified that detail the CIA's relationship with many Nazi figures in the 40s, 50s and into the 60s.'

'My god,' I said, 'When I tell Paul this, he might not be so quick to support the Americans.'

6
The Julius Rosenwald Schools

'Have you heard of the Rosenwald School project?' I asked as I sat down opposite Paul.

'And good morning to you, too,' he said, toasting me ironically with his coffee cup. 'But to answer your question, no. Why do you ask?' He gestured to our waiter and pointed at me.

'I've been reading about it, and it did great things for African-American education in the southern states in the US last century.'

Paul sighed. 'Such as?'

'It built more than five thousand schools, plus shops, homes for teachers and industrial training workshops.'

'Sounds good,' Paul said with a faint smile. 'I'm sure they needed it.'

'Oh, happy birthday by the way,' I said. 'Sorry I didn't mention it when I sat down. We got you this.' I put a small parcel on the table and pushed it across to him.

'Thank you, but it's not so happy,' his said in a thin voice, ignoring the gift.

'What's wrong?'

'Nothing.'

'Are you sure you don't want to talk about it?'

'Yes,' he snapped. 'Go on with what you were saying.'

'I discovered in my reading that, before emancipation, it was illegal for African Americans in the US to go to school. Were you aware of that?'

'No, but I'm not surprised,' he said, and gazed over my shoulder, apparently preoccupied.

The waiter brought our breakfasts and I hesitated, then went on. 'Back then, the Whites were afraid that educating the Blacks would lead to revolt. I paused for a moment and tried to catch Paul's eye. 'And after the Civil War, the African Americans wanted to learn reading, writing and arithmetic because they realised education was important to their economic independence.'

Feigning interest, Paul asked, 'Refresh my memory, when was the Civil War?'

'I'm pretty sure it started in about 1861 and finished in 1865.'

He looked at me, sighed and didn't say anything.

After a brief silence I said, 'Anyway, after the Civil War, attempts were made to redress the inequalities of slavery and many southern states began to give money for public education, but it didn't take long before the White-supremacist politicians began to racially segregate schools and other public spaces.'

'And I guess African-American students had fewer school buildings, books, and teachers,' he volunteered in a quiet, monotone voice.

'That's right! Apparently, at the turn of the century, African-American schools in Alabama received sixty-seven cents per student compared to White schools that got twenty dollars. I hesitated a moment and looked up at Paul. He forced a smile. 'Also, White schools in North Carolina had janitors, electricity, water and transportation, whereas none of those services were available for kids in African-American schools.'

I heard Paul mutter something to himself. What was the matter with him? Had his ivory tower grown so tall that he could no longer see how ordinary people lived, let alone the disadvantaged? I pressed on.

'Also, many African-American students attended school in churches, private homes, and even fields because they were excluded from existing public schools.'

I felt the skin prickle on the back of my arms and neck. My face was suddenly hot with mounting irritation at Paul's indifference.

'Because of the chronic underfunding of public education for Black children, an African-American educator, Booker T. Washington, approached Julius Rosenwald, a Jewish-American businessman who was part-owner and president of Sears Roebuck, for seed funding for schools.'

Paul looked at me wearily. Pretending to be interested he asked in his husky voice, 'So tell me about this Julius Rosenwald.'

'He was from a migrant family of German Jews – a philanthropist who lived in Chicago. He was in the rag trade and his business was a major supplier to Sears, and in 1895, at the age of thirty-three, he became one of its investors. At one time, he served as its president, and then as its chairman until his death in 1932.'

Paul's shoulders twitched and a shudder seemed to go through his thin body as he lowered his head.

'Are you okay?' I said.

'Why do you ask?'

'You don't seem your normal self.'

Paul shrugged. 'I'm okay.'

'We can change the subject if you like,' I said, looking straight at him.

'No, I'm interested,' he said, looking down at his coffee. He sat there, brooding, and didn't move.

'Shall I continue?' I asked.

'Yes, of course. Don't mind me.'

I pressed on. 'In 1906 Sears went public. The float was organised by Paul Goldman of Goldman Sachs. Sachs often stayed with the Rosenwald family at their home during his many trips to Chicago. Sachs and Rosenwald agreed that the plight of Blacks was the most serious problem in the United States.'

'What about Booker T. Washington?' Paul asked, piercing his egg.

'Washington was a well-known African-American educator who helped found the Tuskegee Institute,' I replied, picking at a piece of salmon.

'Washington was born into slavery in Virginia and after the Civil War, he became a teacher. He believed that education could help poor African Americans in the south escape poverty, so in 1881 he moved to Alabama to help set up the Tuskegee Institute to train African Americans to be teachers.'

Paul sat hunched over his breakfast, his thin body bowed, and chewed mechanically, lost in his own thoughts. I felt uncomfortable with the lengthening silence, but rather than ask him again what was upsetting him, I decided to keep talking.

'As its president, Washington raised money for Tuskegee and for other African-American schools in Alabama.'

'I guess Sachs must have introduced Rosenwald to Booker T. Washington,' Paul volunteered. I was surprised he had been paying attention.

'Yes, and Washington had gained the respect of no lesser

person than President Theodore Roosevelt and was able to get financial support from wealthy philanthropists such as Andrew Carnegie, George Eastman of Kodak fame, and Henry Huttleston Rogers.'

'Who was he?' Paul asked.

'Oh, an oil mogul, I think.'

He nodded slowly and began to drum his fingers absent-mindedly on the table.

'Sachs encouraged Rosenwald to provide financial support to African-American education and invited him, in 1912, to serve on the board of directors of Tuskegee, a position Rosenwald held until his death in 1932.'

Paul took out his handkerchief, blew his nose, and put the handkerchief away. He was unshaven and looked as though he hadn't slept in a long time.

'Are you sure you're okay?'

Paul ran his tongue over his lips and nodded for me to continue.

'Rosenwald endowed Tuskegee and this allowed Washington to spend more time on the management of the school and less time travelling trying to drum up funds.' I was silent for a moment.

'You're not interested in this, are you?'

Paul wouldn't look at me.

'What is the problem? Why won't you tell me?' I said.

He looked at me and slowly rubbed the side of his face. 'It's not you,' he said. I heard a brooding bitterness below the surface of his words.

'Then what is it?' I realised that there was something inside Paul I didn't understand. I was not accusing him – God forbid – of anything. But I had known him for most of my life and I still didn't really know who he was.

Paul shifted uncomfortably in his seat. He seemed about to speak, but then, after a long uncomfortable silence, he looked out the window and finally back at me. 'There is nothing to talk about, just continue.'

I remained unconvinced, but we couldn't sit in silence, so I rummaged in my bag and brought out the book I'd just finished. I flipped through, found what I was looking for and began to paraphrase. 'So, in 1912, Rosenwald gave a small grant to the Tuskegee Institute so it could build six schools for African-American students. And... um... these schools were the first purpose-built schools in African-American communities in rural Alabama.'

I hesitated a moment and glanced at Paul, concerned that I might have offended him by drawing attention to his strange mood. I knew Paul bottled up his emotions and I suspected that was why he remained silent.

He forced a smile and said, 'Continue.'

'In 1914, Rosenwald donated more money for school buildings in Alabama. He gave $30,000 for one hundred schools.' I scanned the next page and said, 'When other states heard about Rosenwald, they asked him for money to build schools as well. Rosenwald agreed to give more funds in 1916, and with help from Washington and the Institute, they built two hundred schools outside of Alabama.'

'He was benevolent, all right,' Paul said.

'But that's not the end of the story. Hold on, let me find... Yes, here it is. When Washington died in 1915, Rosenwald decided to manage the growing school-building program without Tuskegee and in 1917, the Rosenwald Fund was created. In 1920, the fund moved to Nashville, Tennessee, and its new employees set new standards for schools. The grants now required White school boards to operate and maintain the schools and the local African-American community and its White school district had to match the amount of the grant. Rosenwald insisted on the match to lock in their commitment to the project and encourage collaboration between African-American and White people in building the schools. Some community members contributed building materials and labour as their match. African-American communities also held fish fries, bake sales, and other events to raise money. All in all, $4.8 million was raised by African-American communities.'

Paul's eyes filled, and he looked away and was silent for a long time. I could see his chin trembling. He took a deep breath and said, 'That would have been an enormous amount of money back then.' He lapsed into silence again, staring at me but not really seeing me.

'The Rosenwald Fund was established in 1917 for "the wellbeing of mankind". It used all its funds, both income and capital, for philanthropic purposes. It donated more than $70 million, which is about $754 million in today's dollars, to educational institutions, Jewish charities, universities, museums, public schools, colleges, and of course, African-American institutions. By 1948, all the funds were gone.'

'You said Jewish charities?'

'Yes, it was a collaboration between African Americans and Jews.'

Paul nodded.

'The school-building program was one of the largest programs administered by the fund. It spent more than $4 million to build 5,338 schools, 217 teacher homes, and 163 shop buildings in 883 counties in fifteen states, from Maryland to Texas.'

Paul sat reflexively eating his food but saying nothing. I realised that, when he was in one of his gloomy moods, there was no bridging the chasm between us. I could let the silence continue, or I could fill it. I decided to keep talking. Perhaps he'd snap out of his mood and we could enjoy our breakfast.

'Many Rosenwald schools closed when the states desegregated public schools in the 1950s and 1960s. Some school districts tore down the buildings. Others used them as community centres, homes, or storage sheds. But most were abandoned and left in disrepair.'

'Are you done?' Paul said, turning to me.

I looked down at my book.

'Go on,' he said, resigned. 'Let's have the rest of it.'

'Well, I was just going to say that the Rosenwald program spent over $350,000 a year in the lead-up to the Great Depression and built thousands of schools. There were real educational gains for rural southern African-American students; school attendance improved and so did literacy. Years of schooling and cognitive test scores also improved. Disadvantaged counties benefited the most. There was even an improvement in life expectancy among Rosenwald school students and more of them were able to migrate to the northern United States.'

'So, is it still running?' Paul asked wearily.

'No, it closed in the 1940s, but by then it had spent millions of dollars in fifteen states.' I scanned further down the page. 'Over 600,000 students went to Rosenwald schools from the 1910s until the 1960s.'

'That's terrific,' said Paul, pushing back his chair.

***

Driving home along St Kilda Road, irritated by our conversation, I thought about Paul. This was not the first time I had seen him despondent. I asked myself, what was it that made him so miserable that he was unable to snap out of it? Was Anna right to be concerned about him?

My temper had not improved by the time I arrived home. Sara took one look at me and said, 'How was your morning, or shouldn't I ask?'

'Paul was in one of his moods.'

'Why was that?' Sara asked.

'I don't know.'

'Didn't you ask him?'

'More than once, but he refused to talk about it.'

'What were you talking about?'

'Julius Rosenwald, Booker Washington and—'

'And their schools project for African-American kids? That was a great program. Do you think it had something to do with what you were talking about?'

'I don't think so.'

'Why not?'

'Paul's psyche is bound up in the Holocaust and he has difficulty seeing beyond it. I doubt that he would have much sympathy for the plight of poor African-American kids. He's like his father in that respect.'

'I agree, he does seem to lack empathy for others.' Sara was silent a moment. Then she said, 'So, what do think was going on?'

'I don't know, but when we sat down for breakfast I gave him his birthday present, and from that moment on he spent the whole time brooding.'

'There was a long silence, then Sara said, 'That's the answer. I bet you his birthday was a trigger.'

'A trigger for what?'

'If you want my opinion, I suspect his birthday triggered a memory of some sort, maybe of Mengele and the experiments, or his dead twin.' Sara hesitated for an instant, then said, 'That's the nature of survivor guilt.'

My heart seemed to slow as I considered Sara's words. 'That never occurred to me, but it makes sense,' I said. 'He shared his birthday with his twin. I guess when you are subjected to such depravity, such torture and evil at the hands of a beast like Mengele, life might have been reduced to simply surviving any way you could.'

Sara was quiet for a moment. Then she said, 'Perhaps. Perhaps Auschwitz was like a university; it would have taught him, and many others, what it can take to survive.'

I nodded at her to continue.

'Some time ago, I recall reading about a newcomer to Auschwitz,' she said. 'That first night when the soup was being served, he deliberately knocked it, so it spilled onto a guard. The guards rushed him. They pushed his head into the soup pot and held it there. They drowned him because they wanted to make an example of him.'

I felt a cold shudder move through me. Finally, I said, 'I guess each survivor responds differently. Some victims can put the past behind them and look to the future, others tend to dwell on the past and are unable to move beyond that. But what has this got to do with what we are talking about?'

'What I am saying is that Paul might be one of those victims who wants to forget the past but can't. Any trivial event like a simple conversation, or in this case, a birthday, can awaken the past, intrude into his thoughts and colour the way he behaves and sees the world.' Her voice was gentle now.

Listening to Sara, I realised once more how lucky I had been to escape the camps. The thought echoed painfully in my head. No matter how boring it was day after day, week after week and month after month in the cellar, it was so much better than what Paul and his family had experienced in Auschwitz.

'It wouldn't surprise me if Paul feels guilty about what happened to his brother.'

'You're probably right,' I replied. 'Even though his brother died of kidney failure on the boat to Australia, rather than in the camps.'

Sara smiled at me tentatively and said, 'Yes, but there is a difference between actual guilt and feeling guilty; the latter need not be justified on an objective basis.'

I frowned.

'I think Paul blames himself for what happened to his brother, even though he knows it is without justification. He is probably plagued by doubt, self-accusation, guilt and shame.'

Why hadn't I seen it before? I shook my head.

Sara continued to speak. 'I'm reading Primo Levi's book, *If This Is a Man*. I hope Paul doesn't end up like him.'

'What do you mean?'

'Levi suicided. In April 1987, long after the end of the war.'

'What are you saying?'

'Levi, like Paul, was aware that he was not responsible for the death of a single person and that his sense of shame wasn't justified.'

I felt my eyes prick with tears.

Sara leaned forward and said, 'Levi didn't harbour hatred for the German people but, at the same time, he couldn't forgive them.'

I looked at her blankly and shrugged.

'He believed that many survivors feel shame at being alive when so many are dead. He says they carry this shame like concrete, heavy and constant.'

I shook my head sadly.

'Initially, Levi wanted to survive to avenge himself and bear witness, but his suicide was sudden and violent.'

'How did he die?'

'He hurled himself down the stairwell in the apartment building in which he lived.'

'That's horrible,' I said. 'He must have been in so much pain.'

'Has Paul ever given you the impression that he might harm himself?'

I hesitated a long moment. How would I know?

7

Hitler's Judiciary

'Good morning,' I said as I pulled back a chair and sat down.

'Morning.' Paul lent forward and squeezed my arm. His grip was warm and strong, and his tone was cheerful. I was surprised by his friendliness, after last week's brooding melancholy. 'So, what's in store for me this week?' he asked with a wry grin.

'I don't know what you're talking about,' I said, feeling slightly put out.

'Come on, what have you been reading? Let's have it.'

'Well, as a matter of fact, I've been researching the judges who did Hitler's dirty work.'

'Oh?'

'Yes. I've been reading *Hitler's Justice: The Courts of the Third Reich,* by Ingo Müller.' I pulled the book out of my bag, but Paul recoiled. 'Have you heard the names Franz Schlegelberger and Oswald Rothaug?' I asked.

'No, who are they?' He sat back in his chair and titled it slightly away from me.

'They were judges in Nazi Germany who were convicted at Nuremberg.'

Paul sat forward abruptly and gave me a questioning look. His friendly manner receded, and he seemed to retreat into himself.

'What were their crimes?'

Worried that the conversation might upset Paul, I wondered if it was too late to change the subject. But neither of us was interested in the weather or what was on television. Paul had never been interested in conversations that served merely to help pass the time, and was awkward and inept at it, so I pressed on.

'Their crimes were many,' I said in a subdued voice. 'But one of Schlegelberger's cases involved the prosecution of a Jew by the name of Luftgas who in 1941 was accused of hoarding eggs. Schlegelberger gave Luftgas a two-and-a-half-year sentence, but when Hitler found out, he said he wanted the man executed; Schlegelberger signed the order to hand Luftgas over to the Gestapo for execution.'

Paul's eyes widened, and his shoulders stiffened. 'Shocking. How do such people sleep at night?'

'I know,' I said, shaking my head.

'And what about this Rothaug?'

'One case used by the Tribunal to illustrate his guilt involved a sixty-eight-year-old man by the name of Leo Katzenberger. He was head of the Nuremberg Jewish community. Back then, the law prevented sexual intercourse between Jews and German nationals, and he was accused of having sex with a nineteen-year-old German girl – she was a photographer. They both denied the charge and even though there was no proof of sexual intercourse, Rothaug made sure Katzenberger's punishment was revised from life to death.'

Outside, the sun paled behind thin, high clouds. Paul put his hand to the throat of his turtle-neck jumper and shivered. 'How do they live with themselves?' he said quietly. 'So, what happened to Schlegelberger and Rothaug at Nuremberg?'

Just then, Bret brought our breakfasts; he knew our usual order.

'They both received a life sentence,' I said after he left.

'What was Schlegelberger's defence at Nuremberg?'

'He argued he had to follow Hitler's orders, even though he didn't want to.'

Paul sat there, staring at me.

'He was one of four Nazis who bore much of the responsibility for allowing the legal system of Germany to be taken over by Nazi ideology.'

'Tell me more.'

After a few moments, I continued. 'In 1941 and 1942, when he was provisional Reich Minister of Justice, the number of death sentences rose sharply. He authored the Poland Penal Law Provision under which Poles were executed for tearing down German posters and other bills.'

'But the "just obeying orders" defence didn't wash—?'

Before Paul could finish I said, 'He was sentenced for conspiracy to perpetrate war crimes and crimes against humanity because he supported Hitler's right to deal with life and death in disregard of the judicial process. By his directives, he contributed to the destruction of judicial independence. And on the 7th February 1942 he signed the decree that imposed upon the Ministry of Justice and the courts the right to prosecute and dispose of the victims of Hitler's Night and Fog directive, which "disappeared" anyone who opposed the Nazis. He was guilty of instituting and supporting procedures for the wholesale persecution of Jews and Poles.'

'Persecution?' A flush spread across Paul's face. 'What about the decimation of the Jewish people?' Paul spat.

'The Tribunal concluded that when it came to the Jews, he was less brutal than his associates, but he could not be called humane.'

'He ignored the judicial process and did Hitler's bidding,

whether he wanted to or not; it is unforgiveable.' Paul said, his voice rising.

I nodded and got out my phone to check one of the sites I'd been reading. Eventually, I found what I wanted. 'The prosecution quoted him as saying, "It should be emphasised... that in the sphere of the law... it is the Führer and he alone who sets the pace of development.'

Paul snorted with disgust.

'Schlegelberger said he didn't join the Nazi Party until 1938, and then only because he was ordered to by Hitler. And he said he never made use of the Party, never attended a Party meeting and none of his family belonged to the Party.'

Paul continued to regard me narrowly, his dark sunken eyes suspicious. 'That's hard to believe,' he said, shaking his head.

'He claimed to have no ill-will towards Jews. He said his personal physician was Jewish. He also stressed that when the final solution of the Jewish question was under discussion, the question arose as to the disposition of *half Jews*. The deportation of *full Jews* to the East was then in full swing throughout Germany. He resisted the proposal to send *half Jews* to concentration camps and said they should be spared and given the choice between evacuation or sterilisation, the latter being a euphemism for annihilation.'

Paul ran his hand through his long grey hair and looked at me in disbelief.

'The Tribunal said that, on retirement as acting Minister of Justice in August 1942, he received a letter of appreciation from Hitler with a gift of 100,000 RM, and two years later Hitler gave him permission to use the money to purchase a farm. Because of this, the Tribunal concluded that he and Hitler had a good relationship, and it was evidence that Hitler had rewarded him for his faithful service.' Feeling my heart racing, I paused for a moment. 'It said he signed the order that allowed German authorities to abduct individuals alleged to be endangering German security so that they vanished without a trace.'

'The Night and Fog directive,' Paul concluded. 'So, what was the result?'

'The judges acknowledged he loved the life of the intellect and the work of a scholar, but said he sold that intellect and scholarship to Hitler for political pottage and for the hope of personal security.'

'And...?'

'And in its decision, the judges concluded he loathed the evil that he did. They acknowledged he resigned because the cruelties of the system were too much for him, and despite its obvious sympathy with his plight, the Tribunal found him guilty of war crimes and crimes against humanity.' I took a sip of my coffee.

'And rightly so!'

'For a man of his stature to remain in office lent credibility to the Nazi regime.'

'And what did the Tribunal say about the other one, Rothaug?'

'They labelled him "a sadistic and evil man". They said he, unlike Schlegelberger, had no reservations about supporting all the human-rights abuses of the Nazis.

'The Tribunal said he identified, supported and participated in the national program of racial persecution and genocide of the Jews,' I said, scanning another site. 'They said his decisions were made before a trial had commenced and he used his court as an instrument of terror.' I went on, my voice cracking, 'And he believed Jews should be singled out for special treatment – he even had contempt for those judges who lacked the will to carry out Nazi Party policy.'

'So, what was their sentence? Were they hanged, or did they die in jail?'

'Neither,' I said with disgust. 'Schlegelberger was released from prison in 1951 and received a monthly pension until his death in 1970 at the age of ninety-four and Rothaug had his sentence reduced to twenty-nine years and was released on parole in 1956. He died eleven years later at the age of eighty.'

Paul dropped his knife and fork and shook his head.

'The violations of human rights progressively got worse as the Nazis consolidated their power,' I said. 'In 1938, laws were adopted that imposed different levels of punishment for the same crime, a tougher punishment for Jews.'

'Naturally,' Paul said bitterly.

'By 1940, sterilisation programs were underway. By 1942, the Final Solution – the wholesale extermination of Jews – was in full swing.'

Paul picked up his coffee and drank. There was nothing either of us could say to that.

'In German law, there was no separation of powers between the executive and judicial branches of government,' I said.

He looked at me curiously for a moment, put down his coffee and said, 'Meaning...?'

'Well, it facilitated the Nazis' racist and genocidal policies.'

The lines between Paul's eyebrows deepened.

'Hitler declared, and the Reichstag agreed with him, that he had the power to intervene in any case. This resulted in any sentence the Nazis thought was too light being replaced by a more severe sentence, often death.' I felt very cold telling him that.

'And what's more, the Nazis assigned a member of the SS to each judge so they could keep an eye on them, monitor their decisions and report back to Hitler.'

Paul's eyes narrowed. Then he leaned forward and hissed, 'Those arseholes thought of everything, didn't they?'

'You'd better believe it,' I said. 'They were on a mission to murder every Jew – and thank God they didn't succeed.'

'Humph.' Paul gave me a bitter look. He was right, it was a small mercy.

'But there's a lesson there for all judges, perhaps especially judges in the US at the moment,' I said.

'How so?' Paul replied.

'Well, Richard Posner, an American judge, put it best in an article in *The New Republic*. He warned against judges being swept up in popular movements and disregarding the consequences for ordinary people of the decisions they make.'

'Indeed,' Paul said. 'I can see what you mean in terms of the judiciary and Trump.'

'But those two, Schlegelberger and Rothaug, weren't the only German judges to support Nazi atrocities. Most of them endorsed the regime.' I opened the book and flipped through it, scanning as I went. 'Müller suggests that most German judges were ultra-conservative nationalists who were sympathetic to Nazi goals and enthusiastically supported the Nazification of German law.'

He gave me a cold, angry look then, leaning forward, he said, 'There must have been some Jewish judges sitting on the bench when the Nazis came to power in 1933.'

'Yes, but Hitler got rid of them, quick smart. Only a handful of judges demonstrated real courage in the face of Nazi violations of civil liberties.'

'I'm surprised there were any judges with the courage to stand against Hitler – no doubt they all agreed with him.'

'One judge who showed courage was Lothar Kreyssig. He

was a county court judge who issued injunctions against sending hospital patients to extermination camps, and when ordered to withdraw them, he refused.'

Paul looked sceptical.

'It's true. He stood up for what was right and was forced to resign,' I said. I decided to take a different approach to the subject we were discussing.

'As you know,' I said, 'at Nuremberg, many defendants argued they were simply following orders – Martin Bormann, Hans Frank, Hermann Göring, Rudolf Hess, Ribbentrop, Albert Speer... not to mention the doctors accused of conducting medical experiments on prisoners, or the lawyers and judges charged with implementing the Nazis' racial purity laws, or military officers accused of atrocities against prisoners, or industrialists who profited from slave labour and plundered occupied countries.'

Paul looked at me with a peculiar questioning frown, as if he was trying to understand what I had just said. It unsettled me, so I changed tack again.

'What's interesting is that the trial raised the question of what responsibility judges have to enforce unjust laws.'

Paul mopped up some egg and hollandaise sauce.

'As a result, the principle established at Nuremberg was that any person acting in response to an order does not alleviate himself of responsibility under international law if he had a moral choice open to him.'

'So, what were the sentences for these men just following orders?' Paul said sarcastically.

'Twenty-one of the twenty-four defendants at Nuremberg were convicted. Twelve were sentenced to death by hanging, four got life sentences and another four got sentences of ten to twenty years, one died before the verdict—'

'That'll teach those bastards,' Paul said.

'But three were acquitted,' I finished.

I saw Paul take a deep, tremulous breath. 'It's bloody disgusting that some of those mongrels got off so lightly.' Then he said defiantly, 'You know that Mengele also escaped justice?'

I was aware the Mengele was never far from Paul's mind.

'What happened to him?' I asked cautiously, although I knew the story in broad outline.

His voice took on a flat, toneless quality. Almost as if someone else was talking through him. 'After the war, he escaped to Bavaria where he worked on a farm. Then in 1949 he went to South America, married in 1958 and became a citizen of Paraguay the following year. In 1961 he moved to Brazil.' He spoke mechanically, his face empty of expression, his eyes dead.

'Paul, are you all right?'

Ignoring my question, he continued, 'In 1985 a team of Brazilian, West German, and American forensic experts determined that he had taken the identity of his Nazi friend, Gerhard. He died from a stroke while swimming and was buried under Gerhard's name.'

I didn't know what to say.

'You can't trust any of them. They're all the same. They're…' and he began to curse them with every obscenity that came to mind.

I sat opposite him, feeling utterly helpless.

* * *

I would think about Paul and our conversation often in the days that followed. This was not the first time he had raised Mengele in our discussions. More than ever, Paul seemed fixated on Mengele and the horrendous crimes that he'd committed on his twin brother and himself.

I wondered what it was like to live with this awareness. No doubt some victims carried anger, others were able to move beyond the rage and get on with their lives. Paul had studied, become a successful and wealthy surgeon, and married. But in recent times, it seemed to me that the trauma of Auschwitz had returned and appeared to be consuming him.

***

At home, I walked through the house looking for Sara and eventually found her on the back verandah doing yoga. The verandah was enclosed, so she could enjoy the fresh air while still being protected from the rain.

'How do you hold those poses for so long?' I marvelled. 'It'd kill me. All those years of yoga have really paid off, haven't they.'

She looked up and smiled.

'Before you ask, breakfast with Paul was difficult,' I said, standing at the door.

'Why? What were you talking about?'

'We were talking about Hitler's judiciary, but that wasn't the problem.'

'Really? So, what was the problem?'

'He brought up Mengele again.'

'And?'

'So, it's difficult; speaking to him is like walking on eggshells. I'm always concerned I will say something that will trigger a bad memory and send him into a tailspin – it's challenging.'

'You seem to share many of his preoccupations,' Sara said gently. 'Did he get annoyed?'

'He became very angry. Red in the face, swearing...'

'Oh, I'm sorry to hear that,' she said quietly. 'So, what do you think is going on?'

'I don't know.'

'Does he seem depressed?' she asked. 'Is he sleeping okay?'

'Now that you mention it, he complained about having trouble sleeping a few weeks ago, and said when he slept, he had bad dreams.'

'Does he still go to the movies or play golf... does he have any hobbies or pastimes he enjoys?' she asked.

'I don't think so. What are you getting at?'

She was quiet for a long time. Then she said, 'Maybe he is suffering from post-traumatic stress. I suspect that's not uncommon for survivors.'

I remained silent, nodding for her to continue.

'After all he has been through, it wouldn't surprise me,' Sara said, sighing heavily.

Neither of us spoke for a moment, then she said, 'Just image the atrocities, the dehumanising conditions, the loss of bodily integrity, the families broken apart, and death everywhere. And in Paul's case, Mengele's operations and experiments, his inability to have children and the never-ending pain and suffering because of that...'

'All true,' I said.

She looked at me, shrugged her shoulders and said, 'I wonder if he thinks about being reunited with his lost brother someday.'

8

The Mitford Sisters

Paul was late, which was unlike him.

I'd just started on my coffee when he flopped into the chair opposite.

'Good morning,' I said. 'Traffic bad?'

'Not particularly. I slept in. It took me hours to drop off last night.'

'That's no good,' I said, noting his hollow eyes rimmed with shadows.

'You? You slept well?'

'Yes,' I said. 'Last night at dinner, Sara and I were telling the kids about our travels,' I said.

'I remember your 1981 trip – Anna and I met you in London, on the last leg of your journey.'

'I'm surprised you remember; it was so long ago!'

Removing his steel-rimmed glasses, he said, 'I remember you forcing us to go to see that musical, *The Mitford Girls*. Did you tell your kids about that?'

'No, that was all way before their time,' I replied. 'Ancient history as far as they're concerned, but at one time I found them fascinating.'

'All I remember is that they were all Nazi sympathisers,' Paul said.

Trying to avoid another conversation about Hitler and the Holocaust, I corrected him. 'Not all; Jessica was a communist. They were scandalous figures – Diana the fascist, Jessica the communist, Unity the Hitler-lover, Nancy the novelist, Deborah the duchess, and Pamela the poultry breeder.'

'Through the fog of jet lag, I recall the musical started with the six sisters singing "Thanks for the Memory" – that song Bob Hope made famous.' Paul forced a smile. It was a sad smile; perhaps our conversation had triggered a memory. He looked out the window and we sat in silence for a long time. I felt awkward.

Outside, the sky was bleak with clouds. A chilly breeze blew in each time someone opened the door.

'Somehow, the six sisters remained legends even after their deaths. I remember reading about them years ago. I suspect it was the trappings and hushed intrigues of the landed gentry that captured people's imaginations,' I said.

'Landed gentry? What—' Paul began to cough; it was his usual nervous cough and I stopped and watched helplessly as his tall, thin frame was racked. He thumped his chest with a fist and gestured for me to continue.

'Are you sure you want me to go on?' I said quietly.

Paul nodded again, his long grey hair falling about his face.

'Well, apparently they came from an aristocratic family and could trace their roots back to the Norman Conquest,' I said. 'And they grew up in a series of country cottages where their budding eccentricities blossomed.'

Paul took out a handkerchief and blew his nose vigorously.

I continued. 'They were privileged, but not wealthy. The girls' education was haphazard; their mother and a series of governesses taught them reading, writing, arithmetic, and French – leaving gaps in their education.' I stopped for a moment to clear my throat. Then I said, 'Owing to the family's limited finances, their brother, Tom, was the only one who had a formal education.'

'And I'm sure the fact that he was a male helped,' Paul said. Then he asked, 'Refresh my memory, what were their names?'

'In order of birth they were Nancy, Pamela, Thomas, Diana, Unity, Jessica and Deborah...'

'A big family for those days,' Paul remarked.

'Their childhood was interesting,' I said. 'Growing up there was a split in the household; some believed in fascism, others in communism.'

Paul nodded, but ate silently.

'When they talked about what they wanted to be when they were adults, Unity apparently said, 'I'm going to Germany to meet Hitler,' and Jessica said, 'I'm going to run away and be a communist.'

Paul looked at me, but didn't seem to be seeing me at all. His thoughts were clearly elsewhere. He gazed out the window, and I began to feel uneasy. But I kept talking. As Sara had often noted, the more nervous I became, the more I talked.

'Unity and Diana did travel to Germany as part of a delegation of the British Union of Fascists, five or six years before the Second World War. Their leader was Oswald Mosley and Diana was having an affair with him at the time.'

Paul glanced at me briefly, then looked out the window once more. I saw that he was annoyed.

'Diana was the unrivalled beauty of the family,' I said.

'Who cares, she was a—'

I raised a hand to cut him off and indicated the people sitting around us. 'Diana met Mosley at a society party in 1932 and left her rich young husband, the brewing heir Bryan Guinness. They had two small children. She set up in a residence on Eaton Square to be near Mosley, and three years after his wife's sudden death in 1933, they married. At the home of Joseph Goebbels!' I stopped, took a deep breath and said, 'The guest of honour was none other than Adolf Hitler. And what's more, Diana stayed with Mosley for the rest of her life, despite his infidelities and obnoxious views.'

'Is that supposed to be something to be proud of?' he demanded. 'Fuck her.'

'I know, it's outrageous! But that's not the worst of it. In 1933, she and Unity attended a Nuremberg rally, and saw Hitler ranting. They were spellbound – they saw in him a man who could inspire a nation.'

Paul's face flushed. 'How can you even say that?'

'It's the truth, Paul; that's what they thought,' I said. 'A year later, Unity went to Munich, took a German-language course near the Nazi Party headquarters, stalked Hitler, and in 1934, met him at the Osteria Bavaria restaurant. She was young, attractive, and shared his vision. What's more, she was conceived in a Canadian town called Swastika and her middle name was Valkyrie! Hitler was superstitious; to him it seemed that he and Unity were destined to meet.'

Paul ran his tongue over his bottom lip. I didn't want to make him any more uncomfortable than he already was. 'Should we change the subject?' I asked.

'No, these women are a disgrace. It's worth remembering that not all the British aristocracy were politically sound, or even mentally sound,' he said with a bitter laugh.

'Unity was a romantic,' I continued. 'Blonde, blue eyed, but also clumsy, naive and stupid apparently.'

'Why stupid? Paul asked.

'Well, for example, when Hitler ordered Röhm shot, along with a great many other officers—'

'The Night of the Long Knives,' Paul said.

'Precisely. Unity wrote to her sister Diana, "I am so terribly sorry for the Führer — you know Röhm was his oldest comrade and friend."'

Paul snorted. 'Moron,' he said. 'Too much inbreeding.'

'Unity claimed to have met Hitler many times; she may even have been part of the reason behind the suicide attempt by Eva Braun, who knows?'

'Who cares? She must have been stupid too,' said Paul. 'It's hard to imagine any reasonable person attempting suicide over Hitler.'

'Anyway, Unity was probably never a serious romantic rival. Unity couldn't keep her mouth shut, so she'd have been a risk to the Nazi high command.'

Paul looked at me coldly.

'Unity was a Hitler groupie,' I said. 'She wrote a disgusting anti-Semitic letter to *Der Stürmer*, signing off *Heil Hitler*! It may have been for that letter that Hitler awarded her a gold swastika badge, which she paraded around in, and apparently once she attempted suicide by swallowing it!'

'What a piece of work,' Paul snapped. 'Pity it didn't choke her.'

'I agree. *Der Stürmer* was an anti-Semitic propaganda rag. I can't quote her letter precisely, but she said she looked forward to the day when the Jews would all be kicked out of England, leaving the country for the "English". She signed off with her full name and said she wanted everyone to know she was a Jew hater.'

Paul started to say something, stopped, then turned towards the window. I could see the anger in his clenched jaw.

'She didn't care what happened to the Jews. Apparently, she thought it was fine when a group of Jews were left on an island in the Danube to starve.'

Paul listened in silence.

'The crunch came when Germany and Britain went to war. Unity went to the English Garden in Munich and shot herself in the head with a pistol Hitler had given her.'

'Good riddance,' said Paul. 'What a pathetic fool.'

'Not so fast. The bullet lodged in her brain, but she survived and eventually returned to England to a great deal of media scrutiny, but her wealthy family were able to shield her.'

'Shame,' he said.

'What do you mean?' I asked.

'Don't be dense – I mean it's a shame that the anti-Semitic bitch survived. They should have thrown her in jail for treason.'

'Perhaps,' I said. 'But despite her involvement with Hitler, Unity was not questioned when she returned to the UK, thanks to the intervention of her father with the home secretary.'

'It's good to be well connected, isn't it?' Paul said with a sneer.

'Don't worry,' I said, 'she got her just deserts.'

'What do you mean?'

'She was apparently left incontinent and childlike. Her mother cared for her until the bullet in her brain led to meningitis and she died eight years later.'

'Pleased to hear it!' said Paul, taking a swig of coffee. 'And what happened to Diana? Did I read somewhere that she went to jail?'

'Exactly right – when war broke out the English rounded up all the fascists, including Oswald Mosley and Diana Mitford, who had given birth to her fourth child seven weeks earlier. They were arrested and held for security purposes.'

'Good,' said Paul.

'She suffered a harrowing three years in Holloway Prison but was completely unrepentant.'

'Serves her right. It's hard to have sympathy for someone

like that,' Paul said, making no apparent effort to feel any sympathy.

'Well, her sister Nancy clearly felt none. She denounced Diana to MI5, and so did Diana's father-in-law.'

'It's hard to understand why Diana and Unity were so dazzled by Hitler and the jackboots and rallies,' Paul said, frowning.

'Who knows?' I said. 'Perhaps Sylvia Plath was right and every woman does adore a fascist, but what I do know is that Unity called the stormtroopers her *darling storms.*'

'The anti-Semitism is less surprising,' Paul said in a subdued voice.

'Yes. Diana confessed to not being "fond" of Jews, and supporting some of Hitler's policies. Who knows which ones?' I said with disgust.

'Shame she didn't rot in jail.'

I could tell from the brooding look in his eyes and the set of his face that Paul was upset. I decided to change the subject.

'You'll be pleased to know that not all the Mitfords were fascists,' I said.

'No,' Paul said quietly. 'You said there was a communist Mitford?'

'Yes, Jessica. As a teenager, she scratched a hammer and sickle into her bedroom window with her diamond ring. Her first husband, Esmond Romilly, was Churchill's nephew, the exact opposite of Oswald Mosley.'

Paul took a sip of coffee. 'Fascists, communists,' I heard him mutter to himself.

'So, when Diana was finally released from prison, Jessica even wrote to her cousin, Winston Churchill, to express her disapproval of Diana being released.'

'In their own way, they were all obnoxious,' Paul said.

I smiled faintly and nodded. 'You're right. Most of them were fascists – Unity loved Hitler, Diana was a fascist, as was her brother and both her parents, and Pamela was a sympathiser. Both Tom and their mother, Sydney, were happy to visit Unity in Munich and socialise with Hitler, along with Unity and Diana. But Jessica, Nancy and Deborah were different,' I added.

'Why do you say that?' Paul asked.

'Jessica emigrated to the United States in 1939 and was a civil rights activist, a great defender of the underdog and a brilliant investigative journalist and writer.' I paused as Bret cleared the table and then continued. 'Nancy fell in love with a French politician and moved to Paris to be with him. They never married, and he eventually married a wealthy aristocrat. She was a really fine novelist.'

Paul looked at me, his face expressionless. 'And the third one?'

'Deborah? She was maybe the pick of them. She was the Duchess of Devonshire. She renovated Chatsworth House and made a success of it as a stately home. But her life was sad in many ways. Four of her seven children died soon after birth.'

'Well, I suppose one out of six ain't bad,' Paul said, and pushed back his chair.

***

I found Sara in the kitchen unpacking some shopping when I arrived home.

'How was Paul?' Sara asked as she rummaged through the shopping bags.

'Not sure,' I said.

She looked up, raised an eyebrow, and asked, 'What were you talking about this time?'

'I started by telling him about last night, when we were talking with the kids about our overseas trips.'

Breakfast with Paul: We Beg to Differ

'And...?'

'The first thing he mentioned was that play we went to see in London in 1981.'

'Refresh my memory.'

'*The Mitford Girls*.'

'Oh yes.'

'So, instead of talking about Jessica, who was a brilliant journalist, or Nancy the novelist, we ended up talking about Unity the Hitler-lover and Diana the fascist.'

'And Paul raised the subject?'

'Well, no, maybe it was me... but he was certainly angry about it.'

'I'm not surprised. By the way, I've been meaning to ask you if Paul has ever mentioned the Warsaw Ghetto and the Uprising.'

'Not that I can recall,' I said, wondering what Sara was leading to. 'Why do you ask?'

'Because his family came from Warsaw, and they must have been in the Ghetto before they were taken to Auschwitz.' Her voice faltered.

'Paul would have been a little boy at the time.'

'That's right, I think the Uprising was April 1943,' Sara said.

'Would he remember, do you think?' I asked.

'I think so, he would have been about six or seven.'

'Strange he hasn't mentioned it.'

Sara stood very still, one hand leaning on the bench. She stared at me. 'Are you worried about him?'

'Why do you ask?' I said apprehensively. 'Should I be?'

'Maybe.'

Having been married to Sara for over fifty years, I knew she had something specific on her mind. 'What are you driving at?'

'I hope he doesn't do what Primo Levi did, that's all,' she said quietly.

'Suicide! Do you really think he could do that?'
'I don't know, but I think it's worth asking him if he's okay.'
'What do I say to him?'
'I'm not sure, but you could start by just asking him how he is, how he *really* is.'

9

The Letter

'Oh, good morning,' I heard Sara say when she opened the front door.

Then a man's voice said, 'Hi there. I've got a letter for a Mr Aarons. It needs a signature.'

'Of course. Where would you like me to sign?'

After a few more moments, Sara appeared at the kitchen door, examining the back of the letter.

'For me?' I said, putting aside the newspaper. A registered letter always made me feel slightly uneasy. 'Who's it from?'

Sara looked grave as she said, 'It's from Paul.'

'That's strange,' I said. 'I don't think he's ever written me a letter – and tomorrow's Saturday, we're doing breakfast.'

She passed me the letter without a word.

I ripped open the envelope, pulled out the letter and began to read aloud:

'Dear Stephen

I'm at our holiday home in Red Hill...

'Ah, that explains it,' I said, 'he wanted to be sure I didn't turn up tomorrow as usual when he's out of town, but I wonder why he didn't just phone.'

'Please,' said Sara, 'keep reading.'

'This is the place where I feel most at ease and where Anna

and I have shared many happy times together. Anna is in Melbourne, but I can feel her presence here very strongly. I can't think of any better place to end my life.'

'Oh my God,' Sara gasped, her hands covering her mouth.

'What?' I looked at Sara, unable to absorb what I'd just read.

Sara sat down opposite me and said, 'Keep reading. Quick! There might still be time…'

I swallowed hard.

'But before I go, I owe you an explanation. It will be easy for you to understand. This is my second suicide attempt. I never mentioned the first failed attempt because I didn't want to burden you, and I swore Anna to secrecy.

'I have enjoyed and benefited from our long friendship. Our Saturday morning breakfasts have become more important as time has passed. But in recent months I have been so bound up in my thoughts I have let you make conversation without offering much in return. I apologise if I haven't been as engaged as perhaps I should have been. I have allowed you to indulge your meshugas because I have felt myself slipping further and further away from life and deeper into depression. I hope I don't sound patronising because that is not my intention.'

I looked up and saw Sara clenching her hands in front of her chest. I ran my fingers through my hair distractedly and read on.

'I'm sure you noticed my brooding over the last few months and perhaps realised that I have been struggling. I know you asked several times what was wrong, or if we should change the subject, and with hindsight, I think we should have talked about something that wouldn't trigger my trauma. Most of our conversations sparked recollections of Auschwitz – the icy-cold, the experiments, the killings, the corpses, the depravity, the starvation, Mengele – those memories now plague my every waking hour, and the nightmares are too much to bear. But that is not your fault, and you are not to blame. These memories seemed to permeate my every conversation. It's like living in a pressure cooker – I've felt ready to explode.

'I can't fool Anna, and perhaps I haven't fooled you. It simply isn't fair to either of you. I can't keep pretending I'm happy. I've tried everything within my power to appreciate every aspect of my life – please believe me, I have given it everything, but I just can't do it. I want you to know that our friendship has meant a great deal to me.'

Sara reached across the table and squeezed my hand. Her eyes were full of tears.

Turning back to the letter, I continued. 'I am certain I am falling into another deep depression, and I can't bear it. The truth is I cannot endure this agonising pain any longer. I don't have the will anymore. This time I won't recover. And so, it's better that I am not here and no longer a burden to Anna. I don't want to go on spoiling her life.

'The act of taking my own life is something I do after deep and thoughtful reflection – I have thought long and hard about this over a considerable period. I believe that I have a fundamental right to do so. It is the right of everyone in a free society. For me, now, much of the world makes no sense anymore. During the war, I was determined to survive to bear witness – if nothing else, I have achieved that. My work is now done.

'My feelings about what I am doing are clear. I prefer a calm death to being slowly devoured, day by day, week by week and month by month by the black dog.'

I hesitated and shook my head. I felt numb. Sara sat still; her chin cradled in her open hand. She nodded for me to continue.

'*I have often said to myself, "why don't you just enjoy life?". And the answer is, I don't know, but I have found it impossible! I'm too moody. I don't have the passion for anything anymore. I have a goddess of a wife who has bucketloads of empathy – she is full of love and joy. I can't stand the thought of Anna becoming as miserable as I am.*

'*I have had it good, very good, and I'm grateful, but in the last many months I've become hateful towards almost everyone. It should be easy for people to get along and have empathy, but it is beyond my capacity to do so.*

'*Thank you for your friendship. You may not realise it, but you have been a great support to me.*'

Suddenly, my voice broke and I stopped reading until I could control myself. I wiped my eyes and continued.

'*Please tell Anna I feel I cannot escape my troubled past – I'm haunted by it, and I can't go through another of those terrible episodes. So, I am doing what seems to be for the best. Tell her she has given me the greatest possible happiness. She has been in every way all that I could have hoped for. I don't think two people could have been happier, until this terrible disease took hold. I can't fight it any longer. I know that I am spoiling her life. Without me, she can build a new, happy life. What I want to say is I owe all the happiness in my life to her. She has been entirely patient with me and incredibly good. If anybody could have saved me, it would have been her. Everything has gone from me but the certainty of her goodness. Please tell her to keep going. Her life will be so much easier without having to worry about me, and in time she will be happier without me.*'

I stopped reading for a moment, unable to continue. Sara was shaking her head.

'*I know it makes no logical sense, but I have never got over *the guilt I carry from losing my twin brother.*

'There's no hope left. So, I must end it now. Nothing on earth can help me. I am content with my decision and feel serene. I have lived long enough – I must have peace, and this is the only way.

'I wish you nothing but joy and happiness.

'And now goodbye, dear friend.

Sara and I sat silent, frozen for a long moment. I felt helpless and distraught and broke into a sudden cold sweat. I stared at Sara sitting opposite me, her face ashen. She looked at me and shook her head, her eyes sombre and wet.

There were no words to say.

Surviving

My Story

In memory of my parents, Anne and Stan Marin

Author's Note

My father—Stanislaw, Stasiek, Stanley, Stan—was born into a Jewish family in Warsaw in 1920. The youngest of three children, he came to Australia from Poland at sixteen, three years before the outbreak of the Second World War. He enlisted in 1942, and as digger Private Stan Marin served for almost four years as a stretcher-bearer with the 2/3rd field ambulance unit attached to the 24th Brigade in the 9th Division of the Australian and New Zealand Army Corps (Medical Corps) in Palestine, New Guinea, and Borneo. While he was fighting, his family were murdered. He never saw any of them again.

This book is my attempt to tell the story of my father and his family, and the guilt he carried. It is a story shared by millions.

Much of the story died with other family members, but I have tried to find the best evidence available to fill these gaps and to preserve as much of the truth as possible. In the interests of telling the story truthfully, some names have been changed.

I remember the place of my birth—Warsaw—as a cold, dismal city. The summers were warm enough, but often cloudy, whereas the winters were long, overcast, windy and freezing.

I was born on the 1st of September 1920. It was a difficult time. Germany was forced to accept responsibility for the Great War and pay reparations to the Allies under the Treaty of Versailles, leaving the economy in ruin. People were starving; the government was in chaos; Germany was forced to give up territory in Belgium, Czechoslovakia and Poland; return Alsace and Lorraine to France; and cede all of its overseas colonies in China, Africa and the Pacific to the Allies.

***

When I was three, Adolf Hitler, then a member and subsequent leader of the Nazi party, was convicted for his role in the Beer Hall Putsch on the 8th of November 1923. The government foiled the attempted coup by the right wing of the Nazi party; Hitler was charged with high treason, given a lenient five-year sentence, then released from jail on the 20th of December 1924 with his political standing stronger than ever. While in jail, he dictated *Mein Kampf* to Rudolf Hess and Emil Maurice, who were imprisoned with him.

Hitler rose to power as the chancellor of Germany in 1933. In February of that year, the Reichstag building was set on fire. A communist called Van der Lubbe was tried and executed for the crime. Back then Hitler used the fire to persuade Hindenburg to pass an emergency law enabling him to imprison many communist leaders, which prevented them campaigning during the election. Although the Nazis did not gain a majority in the Reichstag, it gave them enough seats to pass the *Enabling Act*, which gave Hitler absolute power to make laws and permitted him to remove the Reichstag as a source of opposition.

Hitler put Nazi officials in charge of the civil service, courts, and education. They immediately got rid of judges and banned the unions and any other potential opposition. They also got rid of people they thought were *undesirables*, like us Jews.

By banning political parties, Hitler made the country a one-party state and destroyed democracy in Germany.

Because Hitler took over all state governments, he was able to ensure each state did as he wished and centralise all policymaking. Many members of the parliamentary wing of the Nazi party were demanding that the party carry out its socialist agenda.

On 30 June 1934, in what became known as the Night of the Long Knives, the SS, Hitler's personal bodyguards, murdered about four hundred of their members, including their leader, Ernst Röhm. This destroyed his opponents within the party and gave complete power to the brutal SS. When Hindenburg died on 19 August 1934, Hitler declared himself jointly president, chancellor, and head of the army. This formally made him the absolute ruler of Germany and he became known as the Führer.

Hitler had extended his power in other ways, too. In September 1933 he signed an agreement with the Pope, which allowed him to increase his power in Germany without opposition from the Catholic Church, so long as he left the Church alone.

As far back as the 1920s, the Polish government had excluded Jews from obtaining business licences, receiving government bank credit or public-sector employment. And because the government had limited the number of Jewish students at universities since the 1930s, my older brother Beniek, who had achieved honours in his first two years at university, was unable to complete his engineering master's degree. Jews were also denied admission to the medical and legal professions. Government restrictions on Jewish businesses meant that money became scarcer, wallets tighter and people refused to buy from Jews. My father's business dealing in luxurious imported fabrics—faille and cambrics and duchesse satins—was forced to close.

Life for my family in Warsaw was difficult. Back then I was greatly perturbed to hear the smashing of glass in our street as hooligans hurled bricks through Jewish windows. This was before Hitler was chancellor of Germany, but the city was full of anti-Semitic louts who roamed the streets destroying Jewish businesses, attacking Hasidic Jews, cutting their *payot* and destroying their *tzitzit*.

The far-right, anti-Semitic *Endecja* organised anti-Jewish boycotts in 1934, and after the death of Poland's ruler, Józef Piłsudski, in 1935, *Endecja* intensified its efforts, leading to violence and pogroms. In 1937 they passed a resolution, the chief aim of which was to remove Jews from all spheres of social, economic, and cultural life in Poland. And in 1938 the Polish parliament drafted anti-Jewish legislation advocating the mass emigration of Jews from Poland, the boycott of Jewish businesses and many other limitations on Jewish rights.

* * *

Warsaw made me and undid me. The terror and pain in my story were all due to Polish anti-Semites and the Nazis. Back then, it was almost impossible for a Jew to protect himself against the horrors of the cruel treatment meted out by the Nazis and their Polish supporters. I can still hear my father say, 'The Poles are worse than the Germans.'

One of my last memories of my parents was walking into the kitchen and seeing my mother and father looking at each other in silence. It was 1936. My father was leaning against the bench, his solid frame taut. My mother was sitting at the table. She looked frightened. I knew something was wrong because it was unusual for her to show any emotion.

'Pinkus, what are we to do?' she said, her voice hoarse.

My father turned towards the window, chewing at his lip. For a long moment, he said nothing.

'What's wrong?' I asked cautiously. I felt myself beginning to sweat and my heart was racing.

'As you know, Stasiek, your uncle Nathan emigrated to Australia in 1925, then Aunty Freda and little Anne joined him in 1929, when she was only four...'

Papa drew in a breath, exhaled and said, 'Your uncle Gerber has secured an exit permit and visa to go to Australia. These are not easy to come by, so we must not waste it.'

* * *

I am no longer in Warsaw; now I am on the other side of the world in Caulfield, an affluent suburb of Melbourne. I live in a three-bedroom home with a lush garden and double garage.

I live with my wife, but I feel completely alone; there is no one in the world who knows what I went through, no one who knows the guilt I have carried, not even my wife or children. All of my people—my mother, father, sister, brother, many uncles and aunts—are gone. Our persecutors are now long gone, but I live with them daily.

Today, I feel like an old man, although I am only sixty-four. I am unable to work, due to a series of heart attacks and strokes. I feel like a thing left over, an old man with loose, wrinkled skin and arthritic feet. I sit here in my garden in my short-sleeved shirt and khaki trousers, waiting for my wife to say, 'Stasiek, I've made you some tea,' and that final day when the funeral director comes to take me away.

My wife is brunette with clear eyes, high cheekbones and fine skin. Her good looks are dramatic, and she has always been very stylish. She is mild-mannered and meticulous. In truth she is a gentle person, sweet and caring, but most of all insightful. She reads constantly. She loves memoirs, biographies, and autobiographies. One of the books that she often talks about is Primo Levi's *The Drowned and the Saved*. She says it has been instrumental in helping her understand how our past shapes who we are and our future. But more of that later. She loves the garden and has had a lifelong affection for Australian native plants, especially the banksias, acacias and grevilleas.

No one even knows I have a story. Next year, next week, tomorrow, I will be gone, and I will need a small coffin and a narrow hole. There will be a stone at my head, and I would like my parents' names, Pinkus and Sara, and the names of my brother Beniek and sister Gutka to be recorded there. Beniek was seven years older than me, and in my eyes, he could do no wrong.

It is a warm summer's morning. The sunlight brightens the trees and the sky is cloudless and blue. There is silence all about, save for the rippling of the water in the swimming pool over my neighbour's fence. My hand is good, and I have a beautiful Parker pen full of black ink, given to me by my friend, Maurice, because he knows I like to write. I write out my life on foolscap paper to leave an account, a fragile, honest history of myself, and if God gives me the strength, I will place it in my desk drawer with other valuables, and then I will go to my rest.

***

My childhood memories are happy ones. Often, I sit in the garden among the plants—both introduced and native—close my eyes and remember sitting on my paternal grandfather's lap, before wriggling off it. He adored me. I knew by the way he got down on all fours to play, with his hands leaping at me, teasing me. He had a wicked sense of humour. Then, I open my eyes and smile.

My maternal grandmother was sweet-natured and loving and always maintained her religious practice, going to synagogue on shabbat.

My mother liked to meet my father on his way home from work, and a great pleasure of my young life was going with her into the streets of Warsaw at dusk. It was only many years later that I realised her behaviour was partly due to anxiety, as if she did not trust him to return home safely. Jews were often attacked. With hindsight, I believe my mother suffered quietly under her halo of beauty.

Papa could pop up anywhere in those streets; my mother and I would walk on, each of us searching for a first glimpse of him coming home from work in the dark evenings of winter or the bright evenings of summer. My joy was only complete when I was finally certain it was him. As soon as he spied me, he would start acting the goat. Maybe it didn't befit his dignity as the owner of a large import business employing hundreds of people, but he had that rare ability to let his guard down and play the fool in the company of a child, to be stupid and light-hearted. My father's happiness was a precious gift, helping to buoy me up as my mother's anxiety dragged us down.

As a child, I don't recall my mother kissing me goodnight when she sent me to bed or ever telling me she loved me, and when I came home from school crying, she would immediately dismiss my concerns. 'You'll feel better tomorrow,' she would say.

Perhaps the greatest joy of my young life was sitting with my parents in the living room of our large apartment listening to my brother Beniek play 'Celeste Aida' on the grand piano for our father, a singer who could not be silenced. The piano stood near the heavily draped front windows that looked onto the tree-lined street. Papa sang all the arias from the operas and operettas in those days, standing next to Beniek, one hand on the piano, the other in his jacket like Napoleon, or moving through the air to the cadences of the music. As his voice rose, so did he: arms, whiskers, one foot swinging a little over the old carpet, his eyes brimming with a strange emotion. He had a sweet tenor voice I can hear to this day. Beniek often accompanied him, although I knew he preferred to play Chopin. To me, Papa always sang to perfection, whether it was something from *Carmen,* or one of the many other gems of his repertoire. 'La Donna è Mobile' from *Rigoletto* was one of his favourite arias, and I often heard him sing it when he thought he was alone in his office. His voice entered my head as a sort of honey and banished all the fears of childhood. In the quieter passages, his voice had a most beautiful timbre that to this day I have never heard matched.

My father was perhaps at his happiest when he was dressing to go to the opera. He had a private box at the side of the theatre, overlooking the stage, where he would entertain customers and friends, dispensing drinks and canapés. It was one of his great delights.

Our apartment at 26A Ogrodowa Ulica was in a solid upper-class district of Warsaw and was filled with expensive chintz-upholstered sofas draped in fringed antimacassars. I can still recall the glinting crystal and patterned china in dark mahogany cabinets; stiff, immaculate white sheets filled the linen press, and a row of cream meerschaum pipes was displayed on the wall. The living room was a large, handsomely furnished room with Persian rugs on the floor and sculptures in the corners. The grand piano had been given to my father by a grateful customer who had lost all his money and was unable to pay his account. One winter night, the piano arrived on a cart drawn by a donkey and was carried in with embarrassed smiles by the customer and his sons and placed in our living room. The piano was possibly not worth a great sum, but it had a most beautiful tone, and seemed never to have been played before it reached us, in as much as one could surmise that history from the state of the keys, which were pristine.

My father, like his father before him, was able to play this lovely instrument, and delighted, as I have said, in the old operas of the previous century. He considered Verdi a genius. As there was room for Beniek to sit alongside him on the stool, Beniek, by grace of his love for our father and his own great ability, began to pick up the rudiments of playing, and after my father organised lessons for him, he slowly progressed until he eventually played in the Chopin Piano Competition, without in any way feeling it was an effort or a trial.

Many fine singers made their way to Warsaw when Beniek was a young man and sang in the synagogue on shabbat to Beniek's accompaniment. But none of those singers seemed to me to equal the strange intimacy of my father's voice. And

Beniek often played Chopin at the Town Hall on concert nights. Beniek was able, for a time, to find joy and share it with others in the face of the disasters that assailed Warsaw, and to me he is a true hero. But I'll tell you more about this later.

* * *

It was my mother's forty-third birthday and that Saturday evening I remember as if it were yesterday. It had been raining during the day and the weather that night was humid, not uncommon for July.

My father had arranged cars to pick up their guests. At about eight o'clock, thirty close friends gathered in the living room of our apartment to celebrate. Distant sounds floated through the open windows from the street below, the clanking of trams sailing along the wide boulevard, the faint clatter of carts crossing the paved square and the confusion of bells clanging from steeples and cupolas. From the back streets came the distant symphony of whirrs and thuds from sewing machines in basement workshops in the Jewish part of the city, and the murmur from the *cheder* where small children with *yarmulkes* learned Hebrew at long tables piled with books.

The guests were mostly theatre types, intellectuals, musicians, writers; all of them were known to each other, and they were all, at least among themselves, important. The men were dressed formally in dinner suits and black bow ties. The women wore draped and ruffled dresses that accentuated their curves. Many had dyed their hair dark or wore hairpieces, and their gems sparkled from necklaces, earrings, brooches and bracelets. That evening my mother wore a navy-blue chiffon dress with a white satin collar; it was sleeveless, with a narrow bodice.

The party, which was quite formal, spilled into the library

with its high vaulted ceiling, polished parquetry and bookcases opposite the wide expanse of glass. Friends talked politics, sipped their drinks, smoked their pipes and picked caviar and salmon off the trays being passed around by waiters. My father and mother drifted through the crowd, stopping every now and then to engage in conversation before moving on. All in all, it was very stuffy, but Beniek shone on the piano.

Later in the evening the crowd gathered in the living room to be entertained by a recital, with Beniek at the piano and my father singing. They began with 'The Flower Song' from *Carmen*—a great favourite of my mother's. I watched my father as he stood, his sweet tenor voice flowing without force or constriction. Finally, the last note emanated from his lips and he lifted his eyebrows a little, as though he was surprised by the length of it. He sang beautifully, but it was Beniek on the piano who would have brought the house down in New York or London. After the applause faded, Beniek segued into a simple melody, a call that was answered by a voice on the stairs. We turned towards the door and saw a flurry of yellow lights from the bright candles of a birthday cake that was carried into the room by the housekeeper. Father took it from her and walked slowly towards my mother and put the cake down in front of her.

'Happy birthday,' he said, his eyes meeting hers.

As she bent forward to blow out the candles, my father said, 'Not yet.'

My mother turned towards the camera, and they leaned towards each other for a photograph.

At one stage, I went downstairs. Some guests had gathered in the kitchen smoking their cigarettes. Some were talking with the photographer, some spoke among themselves, and others sat around the table talking about Endecja and the future of the Jews in Warsaw. This was likely to continue late into the night. Mr Peleg was saying that Hitler would invade Poland and annihilate the Jews, but others disagreed. I watched as Mr Peleg and Mr Levy sparred like two fighting cocks. Mr Levy was very persuasive—he had a rare ability to get inside your head—whereas Mr Peleg, who was younger, seemed much more negative about the plight of the Jews in Warsaw.

Much later, I went back upstairs. There were bottles and glasses on tables and sideboards and people were saying their goodbyes, searching for their coats and wraps, and seemed to be melting away. When they had all gone home, I went to my bedroom, sat on my bed, leaned against the wall with a smile, and thought about how wonderfully Beniek had played Chopin and how lucky we were to be able to celebrate these occasions in such difficult times.

Only once did I see my mother overcome with emotion. We were in the Concert Hall of the Warsaw Philharmonic, where they held the Chopin Piano Competition. In every school in Warsaw, piano students tried to be selected for the competition, where they would compete against the most talented pianists in Europe. And of all those Polish students, Beniek was chosen to compete. When he walked on stage his face shone with joy. And when I turned, I saw the same look on my mother's face. He played so tenderly—I remember it was Chopin's Nocturne in E flat major, Op. 55 No. 2—and as he played, I had a strange thought; it was silly, but it seemed as if everything would work out for the best.

***

One morning my father walked casually into my bedroom and said simply, 'Stasiek, you're going to Australia.' I was shocked. I knew my father had secured a ticket to Australia, but I thought it would be for my brother.

'What about Beniek?'

'He's still studying, and anyway he doesn't want to leave his friends; he'll go later.'

I immediately went to the study and looked on the globe and saw a great blue space between tiny Poland and the big island almost halfway around the world. I stared, astonished, until it occurred to me that this would be an adventure.

* * *

On an April night in 1937, a party gathered in our apartment. It was a subdued occasion, the mood a little sombre. On the streets outside, in the heart of Jewish Warsaw, the atmosphere had changed. That elusive feeling of shared nationality and prosperity had withered under the cold hand of want, and the fragile new nation's protector, the defender of the Jews, Józef Piłsudski, had been carried on his bier through the streets of Warsaw before crowds of thousands in stricken silence. At the universities, quotas were set for Jews, who were forced to sit on 'ghetto benches' in lecture halls, segregated from other students; government contracts were no longer awarded to Jews; and the anti-Semitic *Endecja* grew larger every day. But the mood of melancholy in the air did not arise from the problems of the present, it arose from those of the future.

The apartment on 26A Ogrodowa was filled that night with the sound of people talking and clinking glasses. My father's younger brother Julian had returned from Paris with his wife Ruth, for fear of losing their Polish passports, and they had come to the apartment for this special occasion. Julian had earned a reputation as a playboy, but finally married a rich French woman. They had come to visit Warsaw on their honeymoon, and we all went together to the opera in a dorożka, the horses' shoes clattering on the cobbles. Sitting here in the serenity of my garden I am troubled by these memories of the wind ruffling Julian's hair in the open carriage, my mother in her astrakhan coat, Beniek laughing and flirting with the young French governess, Mademoiselle Felicia, and weaving marvellous stories of life at university for her.

Almost sixteen, I was about to set off on the long, unimaginable sea journey to Australia. What were the thoughts of my parents, as they watched me that night, soon to sail away to a distant continent? Did they wonder if they would see their youngest child again? I think of my own children, and I cannot imagine how they felt.

On the day when my parents took me away from Warsaw, I could hardly believe I would leave this world behind me, the Roman amphitheatre in the Łazienki Park, sitting in the big Tłomackie Synagogue at Pesach, shopping on Nalewki Ulica in the rush of people coming in and out of shops, chattering and laughing. It was strange, too, to know that I would not see my family for many years; I pushed down the thought that I might never see them again.

Beniek said, 'I will go to Australia, too, and make my fortune.' He talked and talked with his friends about the things he could do in Australia, how they would have a great farm with sheep and cattle, and ride around on horses all day. It made me a little happier to get onto the train at Gdynia, just when my heart had been starting to sink. Papa was so upset he couldn't speak, and Gutka, who was two years older than me, wept floods of tears. But Mama stood there very calm, and said, 'It will be better for you in Australia. Never look back.' She had made me a little parcel of food for the train—she was a very good cook—but when the inevitable moment of parting approached, I saw tears fall from her eyes.

The time came for me to board the ship. It was a terrible parting. When I said goodbye, everyone was crying. I stood there for a little bit, feeling adventurous and nervous. I was looking forward to seeing my uncle, aunt, and cousin, so it was unthinkable that I would never see my immediate family again.

Even Felicia, our thin young French governess, was crying a little, and dabbing at her eyes with her scented handkerchief. But then I'm sure that was for Beniek's benefit. He was twenty-three, very handsome and clever. She was devoted to her 'little Gutka', who was so pretty and well-behaved, and now almost a woman of eighteen. On certain nights, I knew, when the maid who shared her room was away—for her night off perhaps, or with my mother on a shopping trip—Felicia would invite Beniek to share her bed.

* * *

Standing on the deck of the ship I thought about Beniek. I remembered him asking me to lend him money to build a crystal radio set. I gave him all my pocket money, because he would talk about that radio for hours and all the things he would do, how he would listen to London and Paris, and all the wonderful programs that he would hear: the orchestras playing beautiful waltzes, the comedies broadcast in Polish, and the football games played in Cracow and Wilno. He would keep adding improvements, and inventing more wonderful stories, and borrowing more money. But, of course, there was no radio at all. This went on for months until one day I realised how I was being tricked. I hated the injustice, but I couldn't be angry. In my eyes, Beniek could do no wrong. I think he enjoyed making up the whole thing much more than he wanted the money. And Papa gave me all the money back. He was very kind and hated to see anyone upset.

Now I think of everything I have read about the Holocaust over the years. I am sure that it must have been possible to discover what happened to all these people caught in the whirlwind of history. I think of Sara and Pinkus, with their arguments over gambling and expensive china. I think of Beniek going to university and practising the piano for hours every day. I think of Gutka, about to finish school with her friends, perhaps meeting a young man in the gardens long after I had left, going to see a film in the cinema. I imagine the journeys they might have made; in my mind I plot the synagogue, the warehouse, the flat on Ogrodowa, the tram. I can hardly bear to lose this beautiful world, but I know it came to an end long ago, and with it came the end of my father's and mother's family. I understand what this Holocaust means. I feel the flames licking at the edge of this world.

***

I remember almost everything about my journey. That first voyage from Gdynia to Le Havre, then the long journey overland right across France to Toulon on the Mediterranean. Then boarding the *Oronsay* and sailing out into the sea off the Gulf of Lyon, steaming past Corsica, Sardinia, Malta, Crete, and down through the Suez Canal, passing between rock walls and wide shallow banks edged with dunes, and seeing the occasional small oasis of irrigated farms. Then the ship travelled south, out into the Red Sea, past Aden to pick up passengers and supplies and across the Arabian Sea to Bombay and Ceylon, still part of the British Empire.

I recall my sixteen-year-old self watching all these places and peoples sailing past me as I walked up and down the crowded deck, staring at dolphins and flying fish from the rail. As the climate changed from the northern spring to tropical heat, I wiped sweat from my brow, drank gallons of water, and played cards below deck in the evening.

And on the 25th of May the *Oronsay* steamed through the heads into Port Phillip Bay. There was a crowd at the wharf when I arrived, Aunty Leah and Uncle Jacob Gerber and their daughters, my cousins Nellie and Mary, and my other cousin, Anne, with her parents, Nathan and Freda. Anne was later to be my wife. 'We were all excited, especially me,' Anne told me later. 'The ship seemed to take forever to pull in, and then the crowds of people—pushing and craning to see their relatives, you know how people are. We waited and waited, and we were calling out, "Stasiek, Stasiek," but there was no sign of you. We started to wonder if something had changed at the last minute, and if the letter hadn't reached us in time. But then, as the last passengers picked up their suitcases and bags and walked away, we saw a boy leaning against a post, smoking a cigarette, with just one suitcase in his hand. You looked sophisticated and grown-up, as if you had already seen a lot of things and come a long way.'

When I saw that knot of relatives—uncles, aunts, cousins—on the Melbourne pier, I felt a combination of relief, excitement, and sadness: sadness because I had left my country and my immediate family behind; relief that my long journey had come to an end; and excitement about starting a new life in a new country.

* * *

Today, sitting here in the garden, sipping tea and eating a salad sandwich, I retrace my war years from the moment on 11 February 1942 when I finally walked between the sombre grey columns of the Melbourne Town Hall into the cavernous, tiled room filled with desks and tables and was able to enlist, until the day in April 1946 when I folded up my small pile of khaki clothing, belt and boots, and handed them in at the quartermaster's window.

I decided to change my name when I finally enlisted, and so 'Stanislaw' was transformed into 'Stanley'. Day after day I had tried in desperation to enlist, only to be told that as an alien without Australian citizenship I would have to wait until I turned twenty-one. Sitting in that vast, hollow room at the Melbourne Town Hall, I entered my occupation as 'Cutter'. I had done a variety of odd jobs since arriving in 1937, mainly in the Jewish community in Carlton and St Kilda. I made handbags with my Uncle Leon and started a lampshade-making business with some friends.

The threat of Japanese attacks and invasion prompted many others to enlist. And just in the nick of time. On 19 February 1942, 242 Japanese aircraft attacked Darwin. It was the first air raid on Australia by the Japs, and 235 people were killed in that raid. Occasional attacks on northern Australian towns and airfields continued until November 1943.

With unemployment running at ten per cent, the 'five bob a day' offered by the Australian Imperial Forces represented a low but steady income, without the extra expense of food and shelter. On my enlistment form I wrote 'Jewish' in proud, confident, flowing letters, despite the 'Answer optional' appended tactfully after the question. Under 'Technical qualifications' I listed only '4 languages': French, which I had learned as a child with Mademoiselle Felicia; Polish and Yiddish, which I had spoken at home in Warsaw; and English.

I remember the cold room where I did my army medical examination. It certified me as fit, but only for Class IIA service because of my short- sightedness. Class IIA duties—'specified duties in any unit in which the disability is no bar'—

might mean driving a field ambulance, carrying stretchers, or working at headquarters. I rejoiced at being spared from the killing itself. At the AIF Details Depot in Caulfield, I took the Oath of Enlistment, and was assigned the rank of private in the army, number vx75111.

From the Details Depot, I was transferred to the Australian Army Medical Corps Depot in Wangaratta, after four days' leave without pay. I had only four days to say goodbye once again to the life I had been living, to Uncle Nathan's watchmaking shop in Collins Street, to the handbag factory, to extravagant theatrics at the Yiddish Kadimah, and to painting lampshades in a bungalow with my friend, the brilliant young artist Yosl Bergner.

I think of my three months in the training camp at Wangaratta, for the first time surrounded entirely by strangers for month after month. Letters from my family in Warsaw had stopped coming. Although my cousins Anne and Mary wrote to me regularly from Melbourne, they could not tell me anything about the fate of my immediate family. Ahead of me lay new countries and new conflicts, fighting among men who had lived a very different life from mine.

I think about my transfer to the Sergeants Camp in Watsonia. I was popular—I'd always been good-natured—and I could appear conscientious and thoughtful, even if I wasn't. But I wasn't a leader, someone who would stand out in a group. I was never a rebel, a troublemaker, or a poor soldier, but although I was repeatedly chosen in a group, I was passed over. I knew why. Periodically, I simply vanished. I was 'Absent Without Leave', or guilty of 'Failing to Appear', either for a few hours at a time or for a full day.

* * *

I served as a medic and stretcher-bearer with the 2/3 Field Ambulance Unit attached to the 24th Brigade in the 9th Division of the Australian and New Zealand Army Corps (Medical Corps) in Palestine, New Guinea, and Borneo. I have maintained a grim and determined silence about the war ever since. Sometimes it is easier to unburden oneself to a stranger, across distance and in writing, than to face the enquiring looks on the faces of one's family.

I will try to write the story as I remember it. Even though it is many years ago now, it seems little time has passed. I have been living with this story for a long time, turning it over in my thoughts, day after day, year after year. From the outset, let me say that I hated rifles or anything that took life.

We were camped up at a station called Kildonan, near Goondiwindi, doing exercises, when we got our orders to take ship to the Middle East. A bunch of us had become mates by that time: there was Rudi and his brother Stan Jaeger, Blair Cunningham, and Norm Taylor. We marched for two hours, ten kilometres down to Bogabilla, but when we got there, we couldn't see a sign of the train, and the sky was turning purple over the flats. After a couple of hours, I said, 'Well, gents, looks like we'll be sleeping here tonight.' And one of the men said, 'What, here on the bloody ground?' There was a lot of grumbling among the men, because we only had bore water to drink, which was warm and salty.

About five in the morning, we heard the hooting of the train and we scrambled for our packs, men bumping into each other in their haste. So, we were a ragged-looking bunch who climbed down off the train at Sydney. Some chaps had never seen the city before. We were feeling sort of pleased with ourselves, chests puffed out, marching through the Sydney streets to Woolloomooloo on a sunny morning. And then we got our first glimpse of the boat, the *Aronda,* and our spirits sank. I think the reality of war and what could happen hit us then.

Property of the British Indian Steamship Company, the ship was completed in March 1941. It stood tall, proud, and large; its gross tonnage was 8,328. As the last stragglers on board, we were left to string hammocks or bed down on pallets in the storage hold; it was tight, cold and airless down there. One fellow said, 'Well, chaps, I'm off home,' and the lot of us laughed, but to tell you the truth, our hearts were in our boots.

I can't tell you what it was like in that ship, packed to the gunwales with men, as we turned down into the Southern Ocean and rounded Tasmania (we couldn't go through Bass Strait as it was mined). The waves would reach 25 feet high, and the ship would go right under them. Blair Cunningham came down from the deck, white in the face, and said, 'We were looking straight up into the waves, and I could see the bloody sharks.'

Going across the Bight, we were all nervous. Half the men couldn't stand up for seasickness, and I thought to myself, *There must be thousands of false teeth scattered all the way to Fremantle.* The rest of us were on edge the whole time, and scraps broke out at the least provocation. So, after a while they started locking us below decks. Down in our hold, with not even a porthole for a breath of fresh air, we played cards on the bunk day after day, waiting to get to Fremantle. Rudi asked me how I got to be so good at cards. I told him my father was a gambler. I loved cards and I had done this journey once before, in the opposite direction.

The ship was so battered by the time we reached port that they had a full week's work to get her shipshape again. For us, that week was like an hour to a man about to be hanged, the breeze curling in from the bay, and the sea lapping gently like a puppy. Then, a day early, they packed us back on board, and the men's faces started to get that hunted look they had back in the Bight. It was far worse than before because this time we knew too well what we were in for.

As we pulled out of Fremantle, one fellow—not a young bloke, maybe in his thirties—climbed up on the rail with his yellow lifejacket on. He sat there for a minute and looked over his shoulder at the water. You could see a pod of dolphins in the distance, playing and jumping. Then he turned back to us and fell backwards into the white wake of the ship. It was quiet on the deck; nobody moved. Then I called out, 'Bit cold for a swim, mate,' and everyone perked up a bit. A boat picked the fellow out of the water after a while and took him back to Perth and a great deal of trouble. But I'll tell you, a lot of men on that deck would gladly have followed him.

Let me pause for a moment. Writing down all the things that I have carried with me for over forty years is not easy. Recalling things that happened to me when I was just a young man in a slouch hat, facing situations I could barely imagine, is challenging. But although it is difficult, it is cathartic. Let me take a deep breath, reflect for moment, and continue when I finish my tea.

It was better when we got out in the open sea, calm for a couple of weeks, steaming dead straight across the Indian Ocean. To the east, the Pacific was under threat from the Japanese, following the fall of Singapore in February 1942. That was when most of us had joined up. We all knew Australia was next, likely as not. We looked east as we travelled and spared a thought for the poor blokes in New Guinea, trying to keep the enemy out of Moresby. We didn't know then that it wouldn't be too long before we were there too.

Around us, the ocean was calm, but there was danger below.

One morning, we were woken up by the sound of the ship's horn, and a change in our steady north-westerly route. One of our cruisers and a corvette were circling the ship, searching for the enemy below. We all stood watching from the ship's deck. Something flashed past the stern and a man yelled, 'Torpedo!' Nobody could breathe while we waited to feel what we thought would be the dull thud and groan as the ship was hit and began to sink. But the crunch didn't come; we could only hear the far away boom of depth charges searching out the submarine.

By the time we stepped off onto the pier at Colombo our knees felt wobbly with the solid ground under our feet. Jim said, 'Oh, I miss the rocking already. Let's get back on the ship.' And we all laughed. We walked about three paces before we were surrounded by rickshaw drivers, and every time we turned around there was another face saying, 'Rickshaw, Sahib? Rickshaw?'

Finally, we gave in and got in a rickshaw each, but the drivers got into a fistfight, and suddenly took off in different directions. I had a few anxious moments all on my own in a strange city. I thought to myself, *Well, I didn't endure that journey across the bloody ocean to be dispatched by a bloody rickshaw wallah.* Then suddenly we met up at the corner, and we all had the same expression on our faces. I looked at them, and they looked at me, and the three of us just burst out laughing, and we couldn't stop for ages, and the rickshaw fellows just stood there staring at us in consternation.

* * *

The other day I looked back through the letters I'd written during the war and I was not surprised to see that I never talked about my feelings and impressions. My letters contained dates, places, things like that. It was a bad trait I inherited from my mother. She was a cold fish, never able to share her emotions. As I child I was sure she loved me. Looking back, I think I took it for granted, even though she never showed it.

We stopped overnight to load coal at Aden, at the neck of the Red Sea. Next day, when we woke up, we were all covered in coal dust – black all over. One fellow said, 'Good, now the enemy can't find us at night.' But as it turned out it was more that we couldn't find our own men, because we lost a man overboard that night on the way through the Red Sea. We steamed on up through the Canal to Port Said, where we were put on trucks to Gaza. We expected to be sent up to El Alamein, where Montgomery was to deal the enemy such a stunning blow, but we weren't well enough accustomed to the desert, so they sent us on to Tel Aviv and Jaffa instead. We trained as stretcher-bearers in the hospitals around Palestine. Christmas of '42 we spent in Jerusalem and then went on to Alexandria.

Soon we were travelling in a bug-infested train across the desert. The sand shimmered with mirages that looked just like distant lakes and the heat rose up like a wall. Oil from the engines kept leaking onto the rails, stopping the train over and over. We would have to hop off and shovel sand onto the rails for traction so the train could get going again. There were a lot of Arabs working next to the tracks to keep the road clear for the army, and some of the Aussies would crush up a 'dog biscuit' and throw the crumbs out onto the sand, to watch the Arab boys scrabble in the sand and pick out the small bits of biscuit. The poor bastards were half-starved. Some other men would jump off and take melons from the Arabs who were trying to sell them, and then jump back on the train just as it was taking off. But one time, a chap who'd pinched two melons slipped on the sand getting onto the train and was left behind.

So, I guess that served him right.

After a while, it almost got to be like a game. The Arabs would steal whatever they could, even take our kitbags from under our heads while we slept. One chap woke up in the morning to find that his whole tent had been stolen. They were a funny lot. One day we saw an Arab riding on a donkey, with his wife following on foot. We stopped him and asked why his wife was walking while he rode. He said, 'Oh, she has no donkey.'

One night, when I and a couple of mates were very drunk, among the fleshpots of Alexandria, I decided to get a tattoo. I had requested an outline of the continent of Australia tattooed on my right forearm. As with so many other things in my life, what remained of this foolhardy act of belonging was white scar tissue left behind after the tattoo was removed, which remained clearly visible for the rest of my life. I remember the entry on my demobilisation form included the scar on my forearm; I'd had the tattoo removed before I married in 1946.

Not long after we arrived in the Middle East, the big push started: a massive effort, with four hundred guns firing at once, replaced with another four hundred when they got too hot. But we were part of the 9th Division by then, and got posted back to New Guinea, travelling in convoy on a 45,000 tonner. We had travelled all that way and as soon as the fighting began, we left. We were never told, but surmised the Australian government was worried about the Japs taking New Guinea.

It was just after I returned from Palestine that I applied for naturalisation as a British citizen—there were no Australian citizens at that time. This meant renouncing my allegiance to Poland, swearing an oath of loyalty to the British Crown, and placing advertisements in the daily papers announcing my intention to become an Australian.

In my application, I wrote my name as Stanley, not Stanislaw.

With the legendary efficiency of wartime bureaucracy, my certificate of naturalisation was issued in March 1944, a full year after the application was lodged.

By the time we left the Middle East and our training there, we were not raw recruits anymore, but getting used to the ways of war.

* * *

Nothing could have prepared us for New Guinea. They gave us some jungle training on the Atherton Tableland, but it was impossible, like taking swimming lessons in a sandpit. The greatest danger in Queensland was running into a mad cassowary, but in New Guinea there was constant fear, day and night. Fighting in the desert meant you could see the enemy a mile away, it was all open terrain, and you could see planes approaching. It was hairy, but you knew where the danger was, and what your chances were. In the jungle, you couldn't see the enemy if he was standing a few feet away, and often they were dug in underground or hiding in the canopy overhead.

We landed at Milne Bay in early August of '43. The Aussies had pushed their way back up the track to Kokoda, taking a whack of casualties. When we walked into the clearing station, there were wounded and dying everywhere. Blair Cunningham said to me, 'Bloody hell, it's like rush hour in Elizabeth Street...' There was mud everywhere, up to our ankles, and the tents were sinking into it, even on the timber corduroy bases. The track to Lae was worse, the mud was up to our knees sometimes; it was raining heavily and crossing the rivers was getting more and more difficult. At times, we would have to carry a jeep out of the mud, five of us on each side. The roads would become almost impassable for vehicles.

On the way to Lae, we took a lot of casualties, and the

hospitals were crammed to breaking point. When we got to a new site to camp, we would spray the spot with petrol and light it, to help kill vermin—rats, and such—and set up the tents for the hospital.

We had to bring the wounded men back on stretchers; it was hard work. Four men had to carry a stretcher for a long haul, and when night came the jungle became as black as the ace of spades, with rain falling and mud up to our knees. We couldn't see past our noses. The natives could see a bit better, and without them, we couldn't have made it— fuzzy-wuzzy angels they used to be called. Some nights we had to sleep in the rain, sitting against a tree or lying on a log on the ground. I never fully recovered from living in rain-soaked tents on the muddy ground. It was the worst place in the world for malaria, and many men, including me, became infected during the first few weeks.

After a while, the Japs broke through again, and we demanded to have rifles to defend ourselves. At night we would try to sleep, but we were always afraid that someone was moving in the undergrowth in the pitch darkness. One night, I was on guard with Rudi, his brother Stan, and Blair Cunningham, and we heard a noise coming through the jungle. It started as a rattling and then got louder and louder, until something was crashing through the trees towards us. In a panic, we started firing, and suddenly a mob of wild pigs broke through into the clearing and ran all over the camp; there were pigs running in all directions, squealing and tripping and getting caught in the tents. We started to laugh so hard that a couple of us were nearly sick; the other Stan could hardly speak for nearly an hour, he was just shaking his head and laughing all over again.

No one can really understand what it was like, not unless

you were there. You never forget the cobbers who served with you; no one could make it without mates. Some days we would be walking single file up a riverbed, about 20 feet apart, with enemy in the jungle on both sides. We would feel our hair standing up—we never knew when we would cop a bullet. There were only your mates, and nothing else. You would hang onto them like grim death, and worst of all was when one of them got it.

And it wasn't long before we did lose some blokes. One night we heard enemy planes coming over the mountain. We had dived into a foxhole that the Japs had dug—a hole about six feet deep. I dived in first, and Rudi and his brother dived in after me. 'Watch out,' I told them, 'only one man to a grave.' Then about four others dived in too, and I ended up like a sardine squashed under six other men all night, while the Jap pilot made passes again and again, guns blazing. We lost three men and two were wounded that night. So, they put some new recruits into our unit, who had no experience in the jungle. And that's how it happened. One young fellow was on guard—it was about 100 degrees at night, and there was a pale moon shining down through the trees. James Cunningham and Norm Taylor were sleeping on a makeshift bed of sticks and leaves. Norm Taylor turned over in his sleep and this young chap on guard thought Norm was a Jap and fired. He hit Norm.

I was with the doctor in the operating tent when I heard a shot and a scream. Then I heard Jim Cunningham cry out, 'Don't shoot! It's Norm, he's been shot!'

I helped carry Norm into the doctor's tent. He was losing a lot of blood. Next morning, Norm was sent away to the hospital, where he died of shock. For a long time, we were all very quiet; we didn't know what to say. I thought about it a lot. If I had been asleep instead of in the operating tent, it could have been me who was shot instead of Norm. I wondered why it was me who made it, and not him. He was only twenty-seven years old. The young guy who shot him never got over it—they had to send him home.

After that, I can remember trying to sleep, and hearing noises in the jungle. You would grab your rifle and jump up, still half asleep. Wild bananas grew in the jungle, and when the wind blew, the flapping of the banana leaves would wake us up. We never got much sleep. The jungle is a very spooky place in wartime. No wonder a lot of men came out with bad nerves, me included. During and after the war, I started to swear a lot and it took me a long time to realise my nerves were shot; I was angry, suffering from what they'd now call post-traumatic stress.

Just before midnight on 26 August 1942, the Japanese landed two thousand marines to capture the airstrips and ensure a base for air assistance and to provide naval support for the battle on the Kokoda Track. Eventually we pushed them back, and finally, twelve days after their landing, they evacuated, having lost an estimated 750 men. We lost 161 of our finest. It was the first genuine land setback endured by the Japanese. The allied victory at Milne Bay demonstrated that the Japanese soldier was not invincible.

Once Lae was taken, the 9th Division was sent to capture Finschhafen and Langemak Bay on the Huon Peninsula, fifty miles or so east of Lae. We landed north of the town at a place called Scarlet Beach.

Before the landing, a Japanese soldier was captured, and they got him to talk. He said they had orders to annihilate every Australian and American at Scarlet Beach. So, we were ready for the Japanese when they counterattacked. That night, there was a shipload out at sea coming in on barges, while others came down on foot from Sattelberg. Our motor torpedo boats met them with blazing searchlights and machine guns and the 24th waited for them in the jungle if they made it to the beach. If that Japanese soldier had not told us the truth, we would have been wiped out.

In the dead of night, our torpedo boats were approaching the beach in a blaze of bullets from the Japanese who had made it into the jungle; planes were flying over and bombing us with daisy-cutters (100- pound bombs that could slice clean through a coconut tree). The black sky was lit up with flares and explosions, and men were diving off the boats into the water, trying to get away from the attacking fire from above. Hundreds were slaughtered in the bay and on the beach; it was red with blood. It was a miracle any of us survived. It was known as Scarlet Beach because of red screens used to guide landing craft.

We were on the beach unloading equipment when the Japs came over and fired on us, killing some American chaps. They came so low that I could see the eyes of the pilots. There was a hole dug in the bank, and hundreds of men were running to get into that hole, when a big, black American soldier yelled, 'Move over mate and make room for one of your own kind!' For some reason, I found that the funniest thing of all, and I liked the Yank for it, and we got to be buddies.

Our initial offensive, the Huon Peninsula Campaign, was unleashed by the Allies in the Pacific in late 1943. Over a four-month period it resulted in the Japanese being pushed north from Lae to Sio on the northern coast of New Guinea. During the advance, the 9th Division had to cross several rivers and was slowed by heavy rain and flooding. But we soon regained the initiative and began to chase the Japanese, who withdrew inland towards the high ground around Sattelberg.

The Japanese resistance finally broke during the final stage of the campaign and our rapid advance along the northern coast of the peninsula followed. In January 1944 we captured Sio. That's about the last thing I remember before we were pulled out of New Guinea.

Not long after Scarlet Beach, we were sent on to Borneo. Then back home. We all went our separate ways, but I've often wondered what happened to all those men.

I turned twenty-four in New Guinea. Although I was quiet, I laughed a good deal, and I was good mates with all in the unit. It was a strange time, many years ago, but I think of it often. Sometimes, even now, I wake up in the darkness of a morning and think I can hear the flapping of the leaves, and the faraway booming of the artillery. I often think about the sun through the tall palms, their fronds ragged from gunfire, and the sloping shadows of the jungle rising at the edge of the white sand; the memories make the petty details of ordinary life seem unreal, like a dream.

Anne delighted in telling another story when our boys were young. It was wartime and I was a medic on the front line. She would run to the letterbox each night after returning home from work at the munitions factory in the hope that a letter had arrived from me. She refused many advances from men in the hope I would return from the war and propose marriage.

All in all, I served 1511 days at war, 823 days in Australia, 688 days overseas. But when I (Private Stanley Marin—single, age twenty- five years, height 5 ft 5½ in, eyes brown, complexion dark, hair black, side back right hip scarred, forearm scarred) was discharged back onto the shores of my new country, I had changed. I was no longer the same Stasiek who had leaned dreamily against the post on the Port Melbourne wharf, in my dark corduroy jacket and open-necked shirt, waiting, as so many of my people had waited before me, for a new life in a new country. It was a very different person who stepped onto the Melbourne pier in a khaki drill uniform, with the dust of Cairo and the mud of Borneo in its fibres.

Having returned home, I was discharged in April 1946 and married two months later, on 6 June.

One of the important events of my life was when I married my cousin, Anne. Her father and my mother were brother and sister. Anne delights in telling a curious story about when we first met. I was at the piano in the drawing room of our apartment in Warsaw and she banged on the door. I refused to let her in. She sat on the other side of the door, crying. Eventually, my father came along and opened the door. Anne was four at the time, so it must have been just before she left for Australia. As a teenager, I received this as the gospel truth. It may have been. It was a little human story that somehow was still bound up in her memory and demonstrates the enormous allure I had for her then and always. I was the one she was drawn to.

Anne had dark hair, a soft round face and emerald-green eyes. Her skin was smooth as feathers, and she had a warm, generous smile that no man could protect himself against. She was very beautiful to me – a more gorgeous girl Poland never saw. We married soon after the war and Paul was born in 1949 and Bernard arrived in 1950.

I'll never forget my wedding day. It was early evening at Toorak Synagogue. I was so excited, standing under the chuppah with my best man, Joel Margolis, and watching my bride and her parents walk down the aisle followed by her bridesmaid and flower girl. She looked beautiful in her white lace wedding dress with its long sleeves, veil and train and all its intricate details. She circled me seven times to demonstrate that I was now the centre of her life. Then I did the same as a symbol of the creation of our new family circle. The rabbi made a short speech, blessed us, and prayed for new life together. We placed rings on each other's fingers, and I recall the enthusiastic shouts of *mazel tov* from our guests when I broke the glass.

The wedding ceremony was followed that night by a reception at Maison de Luxe in Elwood. Our guests arrived before us. When we entered the hall, the band started playing and people formed a circle around us and danced the *hora*. Then Reuben Solomon, a close friend and future business partner, and a group of other strong men hoisted us high above the crowd on chairs to the infectious sounds of *Hava Nagila*. Anne and I held either end of a napkin as a symbol of our connection; it signified our marriage contract. After what seemed a long time, our chairs were placed on the floor, and we joined our guests in dancing the *hora*. Eventually, the music stopped and, exhausted, we all sat down for the blessing over challah and a lovely *kosher* meal of chicken, fish, and roasted vegetables.

It was a wedding like countless others, but it meant so much to me after the loss of my parents and siblings. On such a day, I was especially conscious of their absence, and when the time came for me to speak, I said how much I missed them and wished they could be with us. Tears came to my eyes, and you could have heard a pin drop. But I also spoke about how lucky I was to marry such a wonderful person, and how thrilled I was to be starting a new life, in a new country, with her. I truly felt optimistic about our future.

Back then, I didn't realise I would never see my parents and siblings again and I had no conception of the difficulties and heartache that was to come.

It was not that long ago that I sat at the back of a church, listening to a eulogy.

'Les, my father, had a good and undistinguished war,' Robert began. 'Because of a ruptured eardrum and hernia, he was classified as a non-combatant soldier. We went back to Sabah on Borneo together, and twice local blokes came up to me and asked if my father had fought the Japanese. I told them 'Yes—he was on Labuan.' On each occasion, they said to Les, 'Thank you for saving us from the Japanese.' On these occasions, Les became very awkward and seemed bewildered because he really thought he did nothing.'

Les Anderson and I had met during the war, and we were great gambling mates. Our friendship seemed to endure through decade after decade.

At the wake, I began chatting to another old soldier, a tall man with white hair and a smart, dark-blue suit, who knew Les and me in Borneo. 'You know, by that stage,' he said, 'our worst enemy was malaria; you and I had it pretty bad.' I remember when we got out of hospital, we joined up with the 2/1st Casualty Clearing Station, on the way to Borneo. The war was over in Europe, but we were still slogging it out in the islands. In May '45 we rehearsed the landings on Borneo in Morotai, but in the end the rehearsal was worse than the real thing.

'To be honest, we were just waiting for it all to be over. We were stuck on that bloody ship for two weeks doing nothing, trying to sleep in shifts, sandwiched between the landing gear and the tanks. There was a lot of waiting—sometimes it's worse than the fighting.'

The old soldier went on: 'You and Les saved everyone from going bonkers in the heat and the boredom and the stale air with your gambling ventures. Remember that two-up school down in the hull? It was small stuff, but a lot of fun. Then you started taking bets on the boat races (using what beer we had) below deck. It kept us occupied; we didn't even mind losing all our army pay. You and Les were characters, I don't think there's one man among the 2/1st who doesn't remember both of you.'

We were swept apart by the tide of people moving around the room. I thought about what he had said and wondered what strange alchemy transformed me from the quiet twenty-one-year-old immigrant who boarded the *Aronda* in Sydney into the brash, confident Australian soldier, with his tattoo and his gambling, who arrived in Brisbane on 16 February 1946.

I didn't like to talk about my wartime experience. But I remember, on one occasion, I told Anne that in Borneo the surgeons would laugh and joke while they were sewing up the soldiers and amputating limbs. And on another occasion, I recall telling her I saw a man go troppo, put a handkerchief on his head and run into enemy fire.

The other day, I found a folded-up, yellowed piece of paper in one of my drawers. It was a small newspaper clipping, in tiny print.

> **Stretcher-bearers' Prodigious Feats**
> The doctors speak in the highest terms of the work being done by stretcher-bearers who carry wounded from the battle areas sometimes under mortar and shell fire. Two of these heroic stretcher-bearers have been killed and four wounded. The stretcher-bearers follow on the heels of the medical staff and 'leapfrog' from one forward position to another as our advance continues. The unit is so well organised that the medical station can be put in full working order in less than 24 hours. Stretcher-bearers who have done a notable job

since the landing are Pte. Stan Marin, South Caulfield, who was born in Warsaw, Poland. Since Warsaw was razed to the ground by Nazi bombers, Marin has not heard a word from his mother, brother and sister. Then there are Corporal Joe Norris, Cairns, Qld; Pte. Jack Tuttle, Preston, Vic; Ptes Stan and Buddy Hoffman, brothers, Qld; Pte John Wall, Tasmania; Pte Jack Featherstone, Melbourne.

One of the hardest-working ambulance jeep drivers is Sergeant Frank ('Paddle-foot') Norman, Brisbane, so-called because his mates assert he wears the largest pair of boots in New Guinea.

* * *

In 1956, Melbourne hosted the Olympics. The city was decorated everywhere for the Games, as the Olympic torch made its way from fist to fist across the continent. The city was being transformed by waves of migrants from many lands looking for a place of refuge or a better life. They were changing irrevocably the old British colony on Aboriginal land that had been settled by convicts, squatters, and settlers. The Sidewalk Café opened in 1958 and patrons of European cafés began spilling onto the pavements of Carlton and St Kilda, and culture and sophistication seemed to have blown in like a cloud carried by the war.

In July, at his house in Toorak, Reuben Solomon held a fancy- dress party for his friends. Like so many couples across the country who had rushed to get married in the euphoria of the war's end, Reuben and his wife Sela were now celebrating their tenth anniversary. Reuben was dressed as Samson, with a tunic and a huge black mane of flowing locks, and Sela was Delilah, with a plunging décolletage and wielding a large pair of scissors.

At midnight, the lights suddenly went out, and there was dead silence for a few moments. Then the lights flashed on, and a man dressed as a jockey entered the room mounted on a horse. A voice over a loudspeaker announced, 'And it's Cheeky Chap, edging ahead on the last bend, yes Cheeky Chap into the straight, followed by Martaz and Florilles, and it's Cheeky Chap, Cheeky Chap for the win.' The party broke into applause, as I, in a jockey's peaked cap and jodhpurs, climbed down from my precarious perch on top of my two friends who were suffering badly from heat stress inside the horse costume. I went to my wife, who was dressed in the style of the roaring twenties, and proceeded to get roaring drunk.

Today, I am in the lounge, looking at the black-and-white photograph of myself and Anne at the party. In the photo, I look happy, with a blissful, confident smile, perhaps a little more self-assured for the beer I had drunk while waiting for my grand entrance. Anne looks nervous, even slightly disapproving in her flapper costume. But she will not say anything: she will smile and get me home safely to sleep it off.

Anyway, I met Reuben first at one of those welcome parties they used to have, when new people arrived in Melbourne. After that, I didn't see him again for a long time. A couple of years later, in the middle of the war—'41, '42—I called him up when I was going to the Middle East, to ask what I was in for. I was a bit nervous, I suppose. He told me, 'Well, it gets pretty hot round the pyramids.'

A couple of years after the war, I went to him with a proposal: we should buy out his brother Alec's coat-making business. I'd done a bit of work with my uncle in handbags and such, so I could see the opportunity. But, of course, I didn't have a copper nickel to my name. So, I needed him to get terms with Alec, and that's what we did. And we made our money back in a couple of years and sold the business at a profit.

We stayed in business together for twenty years. We were lucky. But it didn't last.

Our Chapel Street operation made a lot of money. Well, that wasn't really business, it was a little venture on the far side of the law, shall we say. And it damn near ruined us both. Names in the papers, police at the house. It was fun for a while, and we made a fair bit of money, but you must know when to walk away.

The sandwich bar: now that was a proper business, and we made a decent profit on it, too. Then we bought another one in La Trobe Street in the city, sold that and started a construction business. And then the nurseries. They were really a big mistake.

It was around then that this picture was taken. Our tenth anniversary. I got blind drunk. I was wetting the heads of my racehorses. I was flying high. Looking at that photo, I can tell I am a happy guy. But later I changed. I wasn't like that anymore. So, what happened? When did things change?

Thinking back, my father died at the age of forty-eight in Europe in 1938. I was eighteen. It was not long after I'd left for Australia. When I was forty-eight years old, I had my first stroke, and my younger son Bernard was eighteen. The ages coincided and I suspect that was the trigger.

But I'm getting sidetracked. Financially, the nurseries were a disaster. It took us two years to cut our losses and sell up. We got back into building and hooked up with Colt & Co. Real Estate in Ripponlea for a couple of years. Then we set up on our own in Jules Meltzer's building. Rent free. I guess Jules took pity on us. The building company wasn't solvent, so in the end we had to close that, too.

It was then that Artie Greenvach offered Reuben a partnership, and he brought me in too, because we'd always done everything together. It was a good deal; lots of potential to build up the business. But it wasn't for me. By that stage, I couldn't make a decision for myself. I always had to rely on Reuben. And I wasn't interested in real estate; I used to sit in the office all day and read the *Racing Guide*.

By that time, I think Reuben had decided he wanted me out. He went and spoke to Anne. Later she told me what he'd said. 'We both know something's wrong with Stan. He's a great guy. You know he's always helping other people. Now he needs to help himself. I think we should buy him out.'

Then Reuben came to me and said, 'I think it's time that we parted company. I want to make you an offer to buy you out.'

What could I do? I felt helpless. And so, I agreed. I didn't make a fuss, just shook hands, and that was that.

But then, at the last minute, I changed my mind. First, it wasn't enough money. So Reuben agreed to up the price by ten per cent. I insisted all the negotiations had to go through Jack Rosenfeld, our accountant, just to be sure there was nothing amiss. Then, finally, on the day we were going to sign, I rang him and said, 'Since it's on terms, I want Sela'—that's Reuben's wife—'to guarantee the sale.' He agreed but, after that, never a word passed between us again.

Thinking back, I treated Reuben like a brother. He had replaced Beniek. It was unconscious, of course. I had looked up to Beniek, listened to what he had to say and relied on his judgement, and I regarded Reuben in the same way. He could do no wrong. So that day, when he walked into the office and said he wanted to end our business partnership, it was more than a business transaction. It was a rejection by an elder brother who, I thought, would always be there for me, a brother who would look after me and protect me.

That incident took me back to my life in Warsaw. I thought

of my father and his gambling, my mother and her fears, and I thought of Beniek going to university and practising the piano for hours every day. I thought of Gutka, in her final year at school, studying long hours, looking forward to going to university.

My wife said, 'Stasiek, you have just had a stroke, how could he do that to you?'

I had already lost Beniek. I didn't want to lose Reuben. But he had cut the umbilical cord. I felt regret for what he had done and the end of the friendship. Had it not been for Anne's insistence, I would have fought to retain our relationship.

***

A few weeks ago, I went to the attic. Hidden among the old journals, articles and documents, I found a box full of old papers and photographs. I took out a small, worn sheet of writing paper, folded in four. Some of the writing was difficult to read, where the paper had worn along the creases.

'To my dear uncles and aunt,' it said, in careful, schoolboy copperplate:

Many thanks for your letter and for the pound you sent me. I am very glad you remember me. How are you? How is business? I should like to see you. I hope that when I finish my school that I go to Australia to be with you and with Uncle Nathan. How is he? Tell him that his daughter is a young Miss. This week she is four years. We all are well. Please write to us every week. Our best regards and kisses to you.

Yours Beniek.

I read the letter over several times in silence. This careful writing was the last trace of Beniek. My uncle Nathan had gone to Australia in 1925, worked hard and saved up enough money to bring his wife Freda and daughter Anne to Australia in 1929. Anne was four at the time, as I think I've said. The letter had been written long before I left Warsaw, and the young miss was now my wife.

I loved Beniek; I loved him very much. It was Beniek who wanted to come to Melbourne after me when he finished university. My uncle was going to organise a permit for him. I remember him at the station when I left; he was so excited for me. He promised to see me again, to come to Australia and be a great success. But it was not to be.

It was a terrible time in 1937; things were getting very bad. Life was hard for everyone, and for Jews, it was worse. My father had lost a lot of money.

Beniek didn't want to leave his friends behind. And there was only one permit. Anyway, I think maybe because he was the eldest, he felt he should stay and look after the family. And so he sent me, his little brother, instead, and thereby saved my life. Not long after I arrived in Australia, I got word the Nazis broke into our beautiful apartment and threw my family out onto the street. I never heard from my mother, sister, or Beniek again. My youngest son, Bernard, is named after him.

I refused to talk about any of this; never spoke a word to anyone, never recalled life before the war. I stopped speaking Polish, or Yiddish. I didn't want to think about it anymore.

* * *

When my father died, my hands were trembling so much I couldn't hold the letter. It was 1938. My cousin Nellie had to read it to me. It said that Papa had had a heart attack. Afterwards I cried for a long time, then I never mentioned it again.

After the war, we went to the Red Cross, hoping they could tell us something about the family. But we heard nothing at all, and after a while we just got on with our lives. Lots of people were in the same position. You just didn't talk about it. So, we just got on with things. And then suddenly, in 1957, those letters came out of the blue from my uncle's wife Ruth in Paris.

She told us that at 11 p.m. on 6 September 1939, Beniek and Gutka left Warsaw. Later, she heard Gutka had married and the three of them were in Vilnius. She said she and her husband Julek (my father's brother) had remained in Warsaw and were sent to the camps where Julek died in 1943. She also said my mother had died in the Warsaw ghetto; she had breached curfew one evening in search of food and had been shot dead by a Nazi guard. Furthermore, my father's second house at Mila Street, as well as the whole Jewish quarter, now lies in ruins. And the letter concluded by telling us that after the war she married a man who took her to Israel and turned out to be a despot; they divorced, and she ended up destitute in Paris. That was the last I heard of Beniek.

I was so disappointed. I decided that was it, enough. I wouldn't rake it all up again. So, I stopped writing. And I couldn't help but be a little bit relieved. I know it seems strange. If I loved Beniek, how could I just stop searching for him?

But I couldn't help thinking about what had happened to him. I wondered whether he'd been packed into a boxcar with another hundred and twenty people: old, sick, children, lunatics or individuals who had gone mad during the trip, only to end up suffering the inhuman conditions in a Nazi concentration camp. Whether it was true or not, I pictured him kicked and punched by Nazi officers on arrival, forced to strip naked, shave his head and wear rags, conditions designed to cause the moral collapse of an individual and reduce his capacity to resist. I'd read that within weeks the deprivations that the inmates were subjected to made each day a struggle for survival against cold, hunger, fear, and fatigue. Food rations were limited to 800 calories a day (2000 were needed to survive). That I knew, but I didn't know whether it had been Beniek's fate.

The Nazis were masters at malnutrition, physical suffering, segregation, maltreatment, and manipulation. Prisoners were told to bring gold, jewellery, furs and currency because it would come in handy. On arrival, it was plundered by the Nazis. All this and the destitution caused a torrent of depression among the inmates. The thought of the Nazi officers refusing to give Beniek a spoon and forcing him to lap his daily ration of soup like a dog was distressing; branding him with a number, like a beast to be slaughtered, was appalling.

I read of the humiliation of having to use communal latrines at mandatory times. In the camps daily roll call lasted for hours and if someone was missing, or suspected of being missing, it could last for more than twenty-four hours. Roll call was outside and when it rained, or snowed, the cold was agonising. If a prisoner was absent, his friends were tortured, and if caught, he was immediately hanged. Any person who did not make his bed on time and properly was viciously punished in public. I don't know if Beniek was in the camps or if he was subjected to all this suffering and degradation, whether he was made to feel inhuman.

Some prisoners, for an extra half-litre of soup, assisted the Nazis. They performed low-ranking functions like washing kettles, acting as night watchmen, bed smoothers, inspectors for lice and scabies, and messengers. I would hate to think that Beniek assisted the Nazis. Although I do understand that the harsher the oppression the greater the willingness of the oppressed to collaborate. Other Jews were *kapos*. They were chosen by the Nazis to help run the camps. They acted as barracks chiefs who oversaw other Jews who were forced to do labouring work and these *kapos* inflicted pain indiscriminately. As a motivation to work harder, they maliciously beat prisoners on the nose, shins and genitals. Other Jews, the *sonderkommandos*, had the job of running the crematoriums. It was their job to direct new arrivals to the gas chambers (most were unaware of their fate), to get rid of the corpses from the chambers, yank gold teeth from jaws, cut hair off women, sort clothing, oversee the operation of the ovens, and get rid of the ash from the ovens. I hope Beniek was not subjected to the putrid smell of burnt bodies.

I don't know if Beniek was caught by the Nazis, and I don't know if he spent time in a concentration camp. Some years ago, I heard from a distant cousin who thought he had died at Treblinka. Most Jews who were taken to Treblinka were immediately taken to the gas chambers and did not spend time in the camp.

I have tried over the years to block out these burdensome thoughts to defend myself against the pain. Other times I have tried self-deception and have unsuccessfully told myself falsehoods, but I have found it impossible to rid myself of these distressing feelings. They have grown worse as I got older and destroyed my peace of mind.

After the war, I asked myself did I do enough to help my family. But what could I do from the other side of the world? Should I have rejected my father's wishes and stayed with the family in Warsaw? I am alive in place of Beniek. It bedevils me, it is buried deep inside me; it is irrational, but I feel guilty. In many ways, I am a guiltless victim. The thought of Beniek being one of thousands of bodies piled on top of each other in a mass grave at Treblinka is devastating.

* * *

I couldn't settle to one thing, and I lost some of the confidence I had had after the war. But I tried my best and we made do. The troubles started, first with the SP bookmaking business, and then with a whole string of businesses, the nurseries, the building, the sandwich bars in the city, and the real estate. I was so sick, all through those years from the war to when I had my first stroke. But I did try. I know I wasn't the most affectionate person, afterwards.

I was at work when I had my first stroke. It was 1966, just before my break with Reuben. He and Artie Greenvach were in the office. I was talking to one of the salesmen when I just collapsed. I remember I was leaning against a partition. My legs gave way under me, and I slid down the wall. It was a stroke, the doctors said. I couldn't believe that Reuben would treat a man that way, a friend. We were like brothers, or so I thought. I didn't know how we'd get through it, with the kids at school. I was terribly worried about being left with nothing if Reuben failed in his obligations. I refused Reuben's first offer because it was much too low. And I asked Sela to guarantee the deal because I knew she had money behind her. Reuben was so difficult: he insisted on taking every little thing to the lawyer, and I was so weak... it was a crime to treat me like that. In hospital, I was so ill I was unable to get out of bed. Then I went home to rehabilitate.

Finally, I was well enough to resume work. I got finance from an investor and started my own building company. But then I had a heart attack. Every day, Anne would come to the hospital, and I would give her instructions on what to tell the contractors on the building site. Then she'd take the train up and arrange everything. If she hadn't, we wouldn't have made it through that time.

I never spoke to Reuben again. Later I wanted to, but Anne wouldn't let me. Not after what he had done. She said she couldn't bear to see me go back and make up. She put her foot down. But perhaps she was wrong. I think maybe I needed a family of my own. I needed a brother, and Reuben was the nearest thing.

I often think about the time I had my first stroke. So much was happening in my life, but I never spoke a word about it to anyone. I didn't want to burden the family, and also, I had been badly hurt by Reuben, who I had treated like a brother; I didn't trust anyone with my feelings after that. So I simply shut myself off from feeling anything at all.

I remember leaving with my wife for my only journey overseas after the war, to visit Paul in Britain. At the airport, I had tears on my face. In London, Paul suggested that we go to Poland to explore our roots, but I was like iron. I refused even to discuss it. It was on my return from London that I had the massive stroke, and soon after a heart attack that left me lying on that hospital bed.

Something had to give. I had bottled things up inside me, and when the aneurysm burst, it almost seemed as though the past was reaching out of to strike me down. They never let go their hold. I had a series of strokes and heart attacks over the following years, and then open-heart surgery as well. The organism was shutting down.

Sitting here alone in the garden, I recall overhearing a private conversation some years ago between my two sons.

'I heard that you went to see Reuben Solomon,' Paul said.

'Yes,' Bernard replied. 'It was strange. I felt guilty, because of Dad. But I needed to know what happened. They were like brothers, and then....'

'What's the big deal?' Paul said.

'I had to cope with him on my own,' Bernard cried. 'You stayed in London.'

'I was going through my own stuff. And it was probably better that way. I only fought with him anyway. You always seemed to get along with him just fine.'

'Fuck you, it *was* a big deal,' Bernard spat. 'Even if you fought with him, you were closer. I resented having to cope with him on my own. It was like looking after a stranger.'

'I don't see why you say that. He was a lot like you in many ways.'

'What do you mean? I don't have his temper, and I'm not a risk-taker.'

'But he was a workaholic for a start. He was always working, even when he was sick. And he was meticulous. Even with his gambling, he kept perfect records of everything.'

'Well, I don't know about that,' Bernard said. 'Maybe with his gambling. It's the only thing he seemed to have any feeling for. He was a cold bastard. He never showed his emotions.'

'No, I don't think that's really true,' Paul said.

'Well, I never once remember him saying that he loved me.'
'No, he wasn't the type to say that. But I felt it all the same.' 'I didn't,' Bernard replied.

'I always knew he was a wounded man. He was fucked – I guess we all are. But I can't say he was cold.'

Then Bernard started on the war, the Vietnam War, and his conscription. But Paul cut across him. 'Towards the end of school,' he said, 'I was supposed to think about uni—a career and stuff. It was all too heavy for me, and I was looking for some way to opt out. So, when the war broke out in Israel in '67, my friend Geoff and I wanted to go over there and join up. As I say, the main reason was that I just wanted to get out of school. But I told Dad, and he said, "We'll check it out.

Give it a week." He called Geoff's parents and organised for someone to come and talk to us about the war. This guy from the embassy came, and we listened. But then, at the end of the talk, Dad just broke down and started crying. He said, "You don't bring up kids to lose them like that."

'He was really distraught, weeping. I never saw him like that before. And so we decided not to go. Geoff's parents were so relieved. They were always grateful to him.'

Bernard seemed really amazed. They sat in silence for a while, and I recalled that stab in the heart I felt when I thought Bernard might be sent to Vietnam.

'Did you know Dad's brother Beniek was supposed to come to Australia instead of him?'

'Beniek...' Paul said. 'I always wondered about that name. It seems to be short for Benjamin *and* Bernard.'

'But I was named after him,' Bernard said, 'so it must be a diminutive of Bernard. Anyway, I don't know why Dad came to Australia instead of him.'

'Oh, I know that!' Paul said. 'Cousin Max said the family lost all their money. So the older brother couldn't come. He had to look after the family. He was studying for his master's degree in engineering, but he had to work in a fruit shop or something. And then, of course, the father killed himself. So he had to stay there.'

'He killed himself?'

'Yes, that's what I heard. Nobody talks about it, of course. Family secret. You know how Mama is. She keeps tight-lipped about things like that.'

'I've never heard you mention it before.'

'I thought you knew,' Paul said as he got up to leave.

* * *

I remember many years ago asking my cousin Nellie how my father had died. 'I know it wasn't a heart attack,' I said. 'I need to know the truth.'

She sat frozen for a long time. Then she slowly turned and looked out the window.

Su-i-cide, she mouthed silently, her eyes averted.

I looked at her face. She seemed almost relieved. That subtle shift in her facial muscles let me see the years of tension and worry that had etched lines into her face. She looked at me very honestly for a moment—it was a look I had not seen before—then she shrank away from me a moment later, perhaps bracing herself for the onslaught of questions she knew must follow. Her shoulders hunched with pain. I could see that she was old and tired. And I could see how much she had loved my father, how much she missed him. I could see how old and how deep this silence was.

'That's all I wanted to know,' I said. 'Thanks.' As we sat opposite each other in the lounge, I glanced across and saw her shoulders relax a little.

In the following week I searched for some clue to help me understand my father's suicide. I looked through book after book to find some reference to social conditions in the period just before the war. What led him to despair? Was it the changing political situation, the growing fear and hatred, the threat of war, the shadowy future for his family, his helplessness to improve his family's situation? Or was it a more personal reason, a raft of gambling debts, a feeling of failure as a husband or a parent, or simple black depression? I felt the strange uncertainty that hangs around the word 'suicide', the fear of instability, madness, desperation. That one word was enough to make it all seem possible.

I asked at my local library for books on Jewish suicide

before the war. The librarian told me about a book called *On the Eve of Destruction,* published in Argentina in 1951. So I tried the State Library. They attempted to locate it but could find no trace. I rang bookstores all over the world. After a month or so, I was completely frustrated and rang the State Library again. The librarian listened patiently to my frustrations and then asked me if I had contacted the Kadimah Library in Elsternwick.

When I rang and asked about the book, the Kadimah librarian returned to the telephone in two minutes. 'It's right here in my hand,' she said in a broad Yiddish accent. 'You want to come get it?'

'I'll come straight away,' I replied.

'But you know it's in Yiddish? You can read Yiddish?'

My heart sank. 'No,' I said. 'I can understand a few words, that's all. My parents only spoke Yiddish when they didn't want us to understand what they were saying.'

'So, we'll find you a translator. You want the whole book?'

'I don't think so.'

'Well, maybe Moshe can help a little bit. What a shame, nobody worries about not speaking Yiddish anymore; it's a dying language. Ask for me, Rachelle.'

When I arrived at the library, she was much as I had pictured her: a woman in her sixties, wearing a sheitel and brimming with Yiddishkeit.

When she saw me, she began shouting for Moshe straight away. He came bustling over, raising his eyes to me and shaking his head. 'Always with the shouting,' he said. 'You need to read this book?'

'Yes,' I said. 'I'm writing a family history and I need to find out about Jewish suicide.'

Moshe registered that with a small start, but said nothing.

The two of them began to pore over the book, perhaps to avoid any uncomfortable conversation.

'Yes, here, a chapter called "Suicide",' Moshe said. 'Beginning page hundred forty-two.'

He started to translate for me. The chapter began by declaring that not only Jews were driven to commit suicide and abandon children on the streets before the war, but also unemployed Poles. The author provided an example of a desperate Pole in Lodz, who killed his children with an axe and then hanged himself. He described the terrible hunger and poverty spreading through Poland at that time.

Rachelle argued with him over some of the words, and their rich, musical voices rang through the library. But, as I listened to Moshe slowly translating the second page, I felt my skin begin to prickle.

'"There was something about the Jewish suicides that made them different,"' Moshe said. He seemed to struggle with his translation. Then he continued, '"The Jews who suicided were not starving. They felt powerless to change their situation; they were tired of struggling with that devil that pushes you to the abyss, that exhausts you spiritually for so long until all your soul powers are drawn out and you are transformed into a little plaything in the hands of gloomy thoughts and seductive spectacles..."'

'No,' cried Rachelle. 'What are you saying? Not spectacles. What is that? Eyeglasses? It means ghosts, which haunt you.'

'Spectres, that's what I meant,' said Moshe, rolling his eyes, 'not spectacles.' He continued. '"Gloomy thoughts and seductive spectres."' He nodded at Rachelle. She nodded back.

'"The Pole who committed suicide because of unemployment is physically exhausted; the Jewish boss who hanged himself in his tallith and tephillin in his several-roomed lodging, is spiritually exhausted."'

'You know what are tallith and tephillin?' Rachelle asked. 'I know the tallith,' I said. 'It's the prayer shawl.'

'The tephillin are little boxes,' she said.

'No, no, not just boxes,' Moshe said. 'They have in them verses from the Torah. They should be strapped to the body during prayer.'

'Yes,' I said, 'I know.'

Moshe continued. '"The Jewish suicide is a sign of spiritual exhaustion; a feeling of hopelessness."' He struggled through the translation. 'It is enough? So, we'll get a translator to do the rest of the chapter.'

'It's a terrible thing to read about,' Rachelle said. 'To think that people were killing themselves, and such horrible things just about to happen. If they knew, I think they wouldn't do it. They would stay alive, just to survive. When you live through the worst, you understand how life is important, no matter what bad things are going on. Life, it's the only thing.'

As she spoke, I could hear a different note in her voice. I could tell that she was there, that she saw some of the things she was speaking of.

'I would like to come and talk to you again sometime,' I said.
'Any time you like,' she said. 'It's a pleasure.'

* * *

I went to see Nellie again, at her home.

'I've been trying to find out about my father's death,' I said, without preamble.

Nellie looked disconcerted.

'I found a book on suicide at the Kadimah Library,' I went on. 'Many Jews felt helpless to improve their family's situation; they lost their spirit.'

'Oh.' She stared at her hands. 'Who told you about Dad?'

'Sulla Savicki was the one who told me. I couldn't bear to talk about it. Pinkus was like a father to me. It was a terrible thing.'

'Remind me, who is Sulla Savicki?'

'She was my cousin on my father's side.' 'Is she still alive?'

'No. It was only when she was dying that she told me. I stayed with her for several nights. One night, it was very late, all at once she began to talk about all of it, about Warsaw and the ghetto, and Sara and Pinkus. She needed to tell someone all the things she'd seen. Frightful things. Many of the things I told you about the ghetto, I heard them from her those nights. She knew how much I loved Pinkus, and she wanted to tell me herself, so I wouldn't find out later and judge him very badly. In the late thirties, she said, things were getting worse for the Jews. First there was the depression, then the anti-Semitism, worse and worse, especially after Piłsudski died. It was hard to make a living as a Jew unless you had saved a lot of money.

'It was then I think that Pinkus understood how much his gambling had cost him. Little by little he had to sell first the warehouses, then the block of flats, and the apartment, too. But he couldn't bear to give to his family the truth even then. Sara was buying new clothes and expensive crystal and things for the house. He sent you, his youngest son, away to Australia. He loved you very much. He knew that he couldn't afford to pay for your schooling, for Beniek's college, for Gutka's wedding dress, maybe even to pay the butcher.

'I think he couldn't bear it any longer. And he felt helpless to do anything about it. It was like that, in those days, before the Germans. People couldn't bear to watch their lives slipping away, losing their social position, letting down their family. So many men just came home one day and killed themselves.'

Nellie swallowed convulsively and after a short moment continued. 'Later, Sulla said, in the ghetto, people didn't kill themselves; it was the opposite, everyone wanted to hang on to life just one more day, to see the Germans lose the war before they died.

But uncle never saw any of that. And if he'd known what he left them behind to face, I know he would never have done it. She said that he hanged himself. But other people said he jumped from a window. In things like that, people don't always tell the details. But the story itself, it was the same.'

I never talked about it. I remembered how, when I received the news about my father's death, I cried. But there wasn't anything I could do to change it; I couldn't go back to help my family; I couldn't ever see my father again. Some family members must have known about it for a long time. I only found out much later when Nellie told me. But they all knew in the family that nobody was to ever talk about it. That's how it was in those days; there were so many things you didn't talk about. I didn't want my father to look bad. I wanted to keep the good memories, so I buried all the other things inside me. And I felt that I shouldn't have left the family, that perhaps I could even have saved Pinkus, and Beniek, who should have come in my place, and my mother and my sister. I felt guilty for leaving the family to fend for themselves.

They were all alone.

As I got up to leave, Nellie said croakily: 'Sulla was the same age as Beniek, seven years older than me. I couldn't bear it. Nobody wanted it to be true. Even now I don't believe it. He wasn't the type. I wish I could have spoken to him, even for only a short time.'

There were tears rolling down her lined cheeks.

* * *

Sitting in the garden, I sip tea, and think back many years to when Paul and Bernard were kids playing table tennis. I recall them laughing and teasing each other over dud shots or misses. I am glad, after all that I have lived through, after all that I have lost, that we were together that night in the house. It's just one moment among a thousand other moments. But this unexceptional moment is exactly what Beniek and I lost, the day I stepped onto the ship out of Poland. I did not know then that I would never share a moment of laughter, of anger, of love with Beniek again. I would have only silence.

I think I was afraid of what I might discover, afraid of what I might learn about what happened to Beniek, afraid of what it might do to me. And afraid for my family.

It's strange. I guess I'm not really a survivor of the Holocaust, because I wasn't there. But I lost more than most people ever do, almost everything I knew as a child, all my family, in one way or another… But I was saved. I know how that feels.

It's like the Pied Piper, I think. I remember reading it to the boys when they were little. He plays his pipe and leads all the children of the town into a cave, and the stone door closes behind them. But just one child is left behind, a lame child who couldn't follow. It's sad.

What happens to the one who is left, I wonder? What happened to me? For my wife, it was different. She was only a child, brought here by a mother and father to live among aunts and uncles and cousins. For me, there was nothing but a silence that only became thicker as the years passed. I was the lame child, sitting in silence, and hearing in my head the echoes of that strange, faraway music.

I often think about the sun shining on the nursery, the music flowing around the Saski Gardens, the flapping of the leaves in the jungles of New Guinea, or the men in Café Scheherazade in Melbourne. I think about why I stopped answering Ruth's letters, why I never spoke about any of these things. And I remember my mother and father and Beniek and Gutka; Felicia and others; my mother's aunts and uncles and cousins on the pier; the line of soldiers walking along the dry riverbed; the shouts of the bookies; and even Reuben, who still goes into his office every day. I will remember Warsaw, and New Guinea, and 18 Chapel Street, and the man in the jockey's costume riding the pantomime horse, and that voice, that familiar voice, my voice in the synagogue singing, *What do you see? I see a rod of an almond tree.*

Aaron's rod was made of almond wood. Although it was cut from the tree, it sprouted again, with new green shoots and small white blossoms.

Sitting here in the garden listening to the birds chirp and watching the dog jumping about, I recall a recent conversation I had with my wife. We often sat together in the living room in the afternoon. She would tell me about her coffee conversations with her friends, and I would tell her about mine. We would share anecdotes about the grandchildren, do the crossword or chat.

On this day, I must have been more morose than usual, because she said softly, 'You are not the only one who feels this way.'

I hesitated, not knowing how to respond. I had always tried to hide the way I felt, but try as I might, it was difficult to smile when my lost family were at the forefront of my thoughts. Many times, there had been nights when I could not sleep. Some nights, I would wake from a nightmare and go into the living room. I would pull up the venetian blinds and stare out the window. On a clear night, the moon would cast shadows on the deserted street and the whole place would seem dead.

She looked at me and shook her head sadly. 'I know life has not been easy. There have been many periods when you have felt flat... depressed,' she said.

I looked at her, shocked. I had not realised she had seen through my façade.

She reached for a book on the low table beside her. 'Primo Levi, Ruth Jaffe, Martin Buber and others have all written about it—survivor guilt. You should have a look; they might help you come to grips with the way you feel.'

I stared at her and did not respond.

She opened the book and flipped through the pages. 'Jaffe talks at length about survivor guilt.' She was silent for a moment, waiting for the dog to stop barking. She ran her finger down a page and read, '"... selection parades, the loss of relatives and being degraded as a human being resulted in... guilt feelings... (which)... persisted or... emerged... only after many years passed."' Her voice became husky, and she cleared her throat noisily.

As she spoke, I thought of my poor mother, alone in the Warsaw ghetto, scavenging for bread. I asked myself what I could have done or should have done. Even though I could think of nothing, I still felt shame; I had left my family to come to Australia.

My wife's eyes, clear and dark, locked with mine for a long moment, and I felt her conviction. Then she read on. '"Holocaust survivors... bear guilt feelings which are gross exaggerations of human frailties, and which are frequently unfounded."'

I leaned forward, and my throat muscles tightened. I felt unable to speak.

'And what's worse,' she continued, '"serious guilt feelings... occurred generally after liberation, when the victims began to readapt to normal life."' She lifted her head and looked directly at me.

I felt my lips tremble. Reflecting on my life, it suddenly made sense. My wife was correct. I had been suffering from survivor guilt. It showed itself years after I left Poland when I was forty-eight and had my first stroke, twenty-three years after the war. The more I thought about it, the clearer it became. I had been blind to it. I wondered why I had never attributed my feelings of shame and guilt to my survival. It was as if I had seen the world till now, not through my own eyes, but through the eyes of others. Now, this new awareness brought with it a sudden lightness.

That night, Anne brought the book to the table. We sat eating dinner in the dining room, and for a long time neither of us spoke. When she'd finished her meal, she lifted her head and said in a quiet voice, 'You really should read this book, Stasiek. I think you'd find it helpful.' Then she took up the book once more. 'For example, Ruth Jaffe says, "... many survivors continually tend to question themselves about what they did or avoided doing or should have done differently. They persist in accusing themselves, frequently without justification. They are unable to resolve their dilemma of doubt, self-accusation, and shame."'

I sat up straight and stared at her.

After scanning several pages, she continued. 'Many survivors felt "... they had no right to live and, above all, no right to enjoy life. Grief for the... dead, longing for the lost loved ones, together with their sense of guilt and isolation, produced a state of unrelieved depression and preoccupation with the past."'

She gave me a worried look, but still I could not speak. So she continued. "'Although the traumatic events seemed not to register when they occurred, they leave deep and vivid memory tracings which appeared and still appear in dreams and fantasies. Guilt... exercises a compelling pull from the past.'" She hesitated a moment and continued reading. "'Many of these people... came to envy their dead for their peace of mind... Having to go on living... they came to develop certain mental attitudes towards their traumatic experiences which tend to persist even today.'" She leaned forward and put her hand gently against my face. Her fingers were warm.

She turned back to the book and scanned a few pages. "'There are those... who... are compelled by an inner sense of duty to remember... There are others who want to forget, but cannot. Any event, even a trivial one, is liable to reawaken the painful past which intrudes itself in dreams and fantasies. Still others have apparently forgotten the past, but are suffering instead from neurotic symptoms which have to be considered as substitutes for the suppressed memories.'"

My face felt hot.

She was silent a moment, her finger tracking down the page. Then she said, "'The largest group... is comprised of those people who have succeeded almost completely in 'forgetting'. But to do this, many of them have had to pay a price, because their memories are merely suppressed, not erased. They function well in everyday tasks, but are impoverished in their emotional lives, since they have to expend a great deal of mental energy in order to hold their disturbing memories in abeyance.'"

That's me, I thought. Even though my brother wanted to stay in Warsaw, I felt guilty about taking his ticket and coming to Australia. The feeling has continued to torment me. I have been haunted by the constant thought that, had I refused the ticket, Beniek would have come to Australia and his life would have been spared.

And perhaps, had I stayed in Poland, my father would not have killed himself. Perhaps, somehow, I could have prevented the deaths of my sister and mother... If I had been with my mother in the Warsaw ghetto, I might have managed to find an egg or a piece of bread for us and my mother would not have been forced to breach curfew. It would have been my task, not hers, to smuggle food into the ghetto. If I had seen a Nazi guard, instead of stumbling and being shot dead, I might have escaped. I deserted her.

That conversation with my wife about survivor guilt made me feel a little better, but it cannot overcome the years of feeling that my own life was saved because I deserted my family and that I have no right to enjoy life.

I had expected to be reunited with my family after liberation, only to discover that all of them were irrevocably lost. And, typically, my first thought had been about what I could have done to protect them and keep them alive. And my second was to wish that I had died with them.

I have lived my life with the dead, and thus I have neglected the living—my own children. I have not been able to give my two sons the love that children need. Perhaps I am jealous of them, having lost my own father, and force on them the lack of love and the sense of loss I have felt.

My family was destroyed. I was damaged... I remain damaged. I can only hope I have not damaged my children.

Quotations from Ruth Jaffe, MD, 'The Sense of Guilt within Holocaust Survivors', *Jewish Social Studies*, vol. 32, no. 4, reproduced courtesy Indiana University Press.

About the Author

Bernard Marin AM was born in 1950 and graduated from the Prahran College of Advanced Education in Melbourne in 1970. He established his accounting practice in 1981 and currently works with the staff and partners of the practice as a consultant. Bernard lives in Melbourne with his wife, Wendy.

Shawline Publishing Group Pty Ltd
www.shawlinepublishing.com.au

SHAWLINE
PUBLISHING
GROUP

More great Shawline titles can be found by scanning the QR code below.
New titles also available through Books@Home Pty Ltd.
Subscribe today at www.booksathome.com.au or scan the QR code below.

Printed in the USA
CPSIA information can be obtained
at www.ICGtesting.com
LVHW032057280823
756540LV00016B/286